Tad Rhymer was the true heir of the vast Rhymer robot works, but his cyborg uncle had managed to isolate him on the remarkable planet Esmeralda. Being part of the Barnum System, Esmeralda was a treasure trove of marvels, most of which Tad could have done without. But to regain his inheritance he had to take his chances in such typical Esmeralda institutions as:

The Church of Aggressive Beatitude
Fetid Landing, Foghill
The Belles-Lettres Cafe & Boarding House
Commodore Snow's robot showbot
Swill, the Magazine of Disgusting Sex
The Ty-gor Triplets, kings of the Jungle
The Underground Rapid Transit System
The Manacle & Fetter Inn
The Blackwatch Plantation Penal Colony

If it wasn't for Electro, the wonder robot, it would have been a wonder if Tad had survived a single day!

Kirby

THE WICKED CYBORG

Ron Goulart

DAW BOOKS, INC.
DONALD A. WOLLHEIM, PUBLISHER

1301 Avenue of the Americas
New York, N. Y. 10019

Cover art by Josh Kirby.

FIRST PRINTING, OCTOBER 1978

1 2 3 4 5 6 7 8 9

PRINTED IN U.S.A.

Chapter 1

The false arm was silver plated and highly polished. It flashed and sparkled, creaking very slightly, as the half-man raised the tinted monocle to his real eye. "Ah, you look very much like him," he said. His thin lips didn't move, the voice came from elsewhere. "Yes, very much like my poor long-dead cousin. And now your bright lovely mother is dead, too."

"Yes, sir," said Tad Rhymer. He was tall, lean, dark-haired. He had turned eighteen the week his mother died. That was a long way from here, on another planet. A long journey through space away.

"Did she suffer much?" asked Joshua Rhymer. When he sighed Tad decided the speaker box was implanted in his cousin's chest—beneath the fluffy lace of his neosilk tunic, probably.

"I suppose she did, yes." His cyborg cousin's appearance was not particularly pleasant to him. Tad turned toward the oval windows of the enormous, chill drawing room. Snow was still falling across the blackness of the night.

Another metallic sigh. "Tragic, very unfortunate," said Joshua, who was, the human remains of him anyway, fifty-four years old. "It might, you'll excuse my pointing out, have been avoided. We, my exceptional sister and I, long ago suggested to your mother that she come here to this planet Esmeralda to live. We several times invited the both of you to make the move, to share one of our estates. We have three in this territory alone, you know."

"I know." His mother had told him a lot about these cousins of his. Tad knew the reasons why she would never accept any of their offers. "My mother preferred living on Barnum, on her home planet."

Joshua scratched at the metal portion of his skull with the fingers of his real hand, producing a hollow grating sound. "Rhymer Industries, as you're surely aware, has branches on all the planets in the Barnum System," he said through his concealed voicebox. "I know Barnum itself well, having journeyed to each planet before my accident. . . . Ah, but you'd no doubt prefer to hear no more about that."

"It doesn't matter." In that same accident, six years ago here on Esmeralda, Tad's father had been killed. "It was a long time ago, and life has to go on."

A chuckling rattled the talkbox. "Exactly, young Tad," his cousin said approvingly. "No matter what happens, no matter how sad events may seem at the moment, Rhymer Industries goes on. It must."

"I imagined you'd feel that way, Cousin Joshua." Tad, very sleepy, moved closer to one of the tinted oval windows. Nothing out there except flat fields and a few of those squat trees which were apparently native to this territory. The snow had long ago covered the blank fields. "I wonder if maybe I can go to bed now."

After a little more chuckling and then some creaking, Joshua, on his flesh and bone leg and his metal and plastic leg, came tottering toward him. "I'm afraid, Tad, you've a bit more traveling to do before you bed down for the night."

He turned to face his approaching cousin. "I'm not staying here with you?"

"I'm sorry, no. Did my people who met you at the spaceport give you such an impression?"

"No, but I thought . . . the impression our attorney gave me was that I was to come to the Aurora Territory, here on the planet Esmeralda, to live with you and Cousin Cornelia."

Joshua's gleaming arm gave off a high-pitched squeak as he put his false hand on Tad's shoulder. "My sister and I would surely like to have you here with us all the time, Tad," he said. "However, *ruzzle muzzle bingle burzz muzz.*"

"Beg pardon?"

Joshua let go the young man, dealt himself several resounding thumps on the chest. "For a Rhymer Industries product this talker of mine doesn't always function as it should. There. I think that's back in first-class shape. How's it sound to you, lad?"

"About as usual I guess," answered Tad. "Where am I going to stay, then?"

"Well, quite obviously an heir to the Rhymer Industries holdings, a young fellow who will someday, I sincerely hope, be a full partner in the organization, such a young fellow has to live in style," explained his cousin. "Therefore we *ruzzle wuzzle rumz bumz.*" With a shake of his head, Joshua began again to pound at his chest.

"I want Phix and Maresca at our Talker Plant fired

no later than Monday next." A thin, dead-white woman was standing in the far doorway. "This continual muzzling-wuzzling is enough to set my—"

"Phix is a competent man, Cornelia," said Joshua, his talking mechanism back to functioning properly. "Tad, this is your Cousin Cornelia. Are you feeling better, dear?"

"No worse," replied Tad's gaunt fifty-one-year-old cousin while very slowly advancing in his direction. "All the noise of this young man's tardy arrival, coupled with that squawking and bawling coming out of your talker . . . it adds up to very little peace in my sickbed. I won't touch you, Thadeus. I'm suffering through a terrible bout of snerg flu."

"A snerg is a very unpleasant little animal," amplified Joshua. "Snerg flu is named after it."

"Seems appropriate." Tad put a hand over his mouth in time to mask a yawn.

"Can this be a sample of your flippancy, Thadeus?" asked the white-clad Cornelia. "We were considerably upset to come upon a rather thick section in your dossier which detailed your career of sarcasm and wisecracking in school and elsewhere. I trust you'll outgrow the habit after you've spent some time at Foghill."

"Sounds likely," said Tad, yawning. "Is Foghill where I'm going to live?"

"Haven't you ever explained things to the boy, Joshua?"

"I was in the process, Cornelia, I was in the process when my talker began acting up."

"You really—if you ever paid the least attention to me at all—ought to go into our Skyport factory for a good thorough overhaul. Have a new talker installed, a new arm which won't make noises like a stuck quilp every time you—"

"A quilp is a chubby little beast huntsmen on Esmeralda are fond of hunting with spears," Cousin Joshua informed Tad. "Though the last time I stuck one it certainly didn't—"

"I'd have them do something with your eye, too."

"My eye?"

"It's been growing increasingly unbelievable, Josh," his sister told him, with a quick, sad shake of her head. "Now, then, Thadeus, you'd best venture out to the air platform. They'll be wondering about you at Foghill."

"Who'll be wondering?" asked Tad. "Will I be living with servants at Foghill or what?"

"This is truly going to be a wonderful experience for you," Cousin Joshua promised. "A chance to learn about many of our better-selling Rhymer Industries products."

"You mean Foghill is staffed entirely with robots, androids and servos?"

"Not entirely, lad. There is the estate manager, Mr. Hohl. He's human."

"I wouldn't exactly classify Hohl as human," said Cousin Cornelia.

Chapter 2

Tad found the robot, the robot which would change everything, late in the afternoon of his thirteenth day at Foghill. He knew for certain it was the thirteenth day because he was counting off each long bleak and lonesome day he spent at the place. He had been promised he'd be allowed to start school again when the next semester started at the area academy. That was still twenty-six days up ahead.

Foghill came by its name because, simply, it sat on a low dismal hill and was almost continually shrouded in thick prickly fog. High black trees filled most of the ten acres inside the high stone walls which closed in the estate grounds. A swampy lake lay at the foot of the hill and beyond that rose more trees, mile after dreary mile, on the rare day when you could see them at all, of stiff dark-limbed dark-leafed trees.

The only visitor to Foghill during Tad's first thirteen days was Reverend Dimchurch. A very old, very thin lizard man, the reverend was in charge of the

Church of Aggressive Beatitude in Fog Hollow, some fifteen miles to the South. He wore a faded purple three-piece priest suit, traveled in a small gunmetal robotcart.

On this thirteenth day the reverend came rolling through the high gates of Foghill in mid-afternoon. He had a purple scarf wrapped around his scaly green neck. "Bit of a chill in the air today, eh?" he remarked when he noticed Tad wandering on a nearby path.

"Same as always." Tad was moping in the vicinity of one of the long-abandoned experimental greenhouses.

Reverend Dimchurch rolled off the gritty path and then across the overgrown lawn. "I hate to see you mope your youth away, Tad," he said. "Are we not told, for instance, in St. Reptillicus' 14th Epistle of the Milmans, 'Youth is like the bag the ice cubes come in'?"

Tad frowned. "I don't think I quite understand that one, reverend."

"Well, it's possible St. Reptillicus' well-known fondness for sending out for liquor colored some of his later epistles," the lizard priest admitted. "The point is, you must cheer up, enjoy yourself."

"Little tough to do that hereabouts."

Reverend Dimchurch, drumming his green fingertips on the edge of his cart, glanced around. He saw mostly fog. "A dismal setting, agreed. Once, though, good times were often had here. For as St. Reptillicus tells us, 'The swizzle stick oft . . .' Well, we'll skip that. The point is, Foghill was once a much happier place."

"Did you know the people who used to live here—my other cousins, I mean?" Tad had been able to learn this much, that two other members of the Rhymer family had resided at the place as recently as six years ago. Then they'd died, in some sort of accident. Another accident, and two more deaths, at the same time his father had died.

"Yes, I knew Cosmo and Alice quite well," replied Reverend Dimchurch. "Hadn't I mentioned that before? I suppose not, since my business calls on your Mr. Hohl tend to distract me considerably."

Tad stepped nearer the robotcart. "What exactly is you business with Hohl?"

The purple muffler was lifted up to wipe at the green lips. "Ah, my boy, you have youth's knack for asking direct questions," he mumbled. "Well, may St. Serpentine bless and forgive me, but I must defer the explanation to a later date."

"Okay, but tell me about Mr. and Mrs. Rhymer, Cosmo and Alice."

"Very likeable people, very cordial." The lizard man's tongue unrolled out between his teeth as he smiled. "And that all-purpose robot servant of theirs . . . a delightful fellow, albeit somewhat arrogant and prideful. He wasn't on the market, not a real Rhymer Industries product, but rather a one-of-a-kind mechanism which your Cousin Cosmo built himself right here at Foghill."

"What do you mean here? There's not a lab or a workshop here," said Tad, glancing around at the shrouding fog. "I know because I'd love to have someplace to tinker and fool around in. I asked Hohl and he told me there weren't any."

Dimchurch said, "There most certainly was a very well-equipped workshop. Many's the afternoon I spent there watching your late cousin at work and debating with him the dubious details of some of St. Reptillicus' more suspect miracles."

Tad jumped forward, caught the lizard priest's arm. "Where was the workshop?"

"Well, my boy, as I recollect, Cosmo had his facility underground, beneath one of the warehouses yonder," said the reverend, eyes narrowed in remembering. "Beneath Warehouse 6, I do believe, though it might have—"

"Hey, Dimchurch, you doddering old pile of creepy green garbage! Where the gung are you?"

Someone was bellowing in the fog, stomping his way. They both knew who it was.

"I'd better roll along to my meeting with your Mr. Hohl," said the lizard priest.

"Are you flapping your ugly green jaw with that skinny, lop-eared guest of mine? If you are, I'll rend both of you simps into bits and pieces."

"Has he ever struck you?" the reverend inquired quietly.

"Nope, he only yells."

From out of the fog bounded a large human-type. He was wide in the shoulders, huge in the chest, hairy. "So! A couple of wall-eyed ninnies I find here wasting and frittering precious time. Thadeus, go to your room! As for you, Dimchurch, I've half a mind to crumble that silly cart of yours into a ball and stuff it up your nork." Hohl took three more steps, halted, swaying slightly. "Say, whatever made me have an outburst like this? Forgive me, won't you?" From a flap-pocket in his one-piece orange worksuit the big man extracted a blue capsule. After swallowing it, he smiled mildly at both of them. "Must be my allergies making me cranky once again. Well, let's trot along to my office, shall we, dear reverend? I've got my butler 'bot brewing a pot of peppermint tea. Your very favorite, is it not?"

"Why, yes, Mr. Hohl."

Hohl beamed a benevolent smile at Tad before he and the lizard priest went away into the fog.

Tad waited three long anxious minutes before running across the fogbound estate to Warehouse 6.

He hadn't expected a robot.

Tad didn't even notice him at first. Most of the light strips crisscrossing the high ceiling of the large underground lab-workshop didn't work anymore. There were splotches of light amid great patches of darkness. "They could be fixed without much trouble," he said to himself, squinting up at the dusty lengths of neoplaz. He could do it with a little time and a few tools. Tad was fond of tinkering, he liked to fix things, to attempt to construct gadgets and mechanisms of his own.

More than enough tools and equipment here in his late Cousin Cosmo's work lab. The nearest table, for instance, held an array of neatly compartmented lecdrills, power-drivers and automallets. Farther along sat a scanner, festooned with spider webs of a brilliant orange shade. "Hey, and there's a 'fuge.' "

That was something he'd never been able to afford back home. Tad wasn't yet completely clear on how the Rhymer Industries profits were split up. After his mother died there had been very little money left in any of their bankcomp accounts. That was still something he had to go into with Cousin Joshua. The lawyer, back home on Barnum, had said he hadn't been able to find out all about the situation. Tad frowned, wondering if their attorney had been exactly truthful. But he let the newly discovered lab and its equipment distract him.

If Hohl didn't foul things up, Tad would have something to do, something to fill the long misty hours at Foghill.

After stroking the side of the scanner, brushing away the glistening orange cobwebs, Tad moved on. There was a damp, raw earth smell all around. He noticed underfoot, as he crossed into a dark unlit section of the lab, swirls of purplish mildew fuzzing the plyo floor.

Tad stopped suddenly still, hair at the nape of his neck bristling. Something had moved in the shadows. Then the pure-white rat went darting across the aisle between the lab tables. Laughing at himself, Tad realized what it was he'd heard. He resumed his exploring.

He found Electro in a far corner, though he didn't know the robot's name then and Electro was in no shape to introduce himself.

"It's almost . . . almost like . . . a murder," Tad murmured, kneeling beside the mechanism.

The robot was sitting slumped in a dark corner, legs wide-spread and arms dangling. He was humanoid in shape and facial features, and if he's been able to rise and stand he's have measured well over seven feet in height. Orginally Electro had been chrome plated, but he was tarnished now and stretches of his once-bright exterior were pocked. Green, yellow and orange spider webs laced his hung-down head, his splayed fingers, and elbows and knees.

But someone had done more than simply abandon the robot. The control panel in his wide chest had been roughly ripped open and his complex inner workings smashed with an automallet of some sort. Tiny wires, twists of plaztubing, slivers of neoglass, mangled bits of printed circuitry dribbled out of the gape.

This has got to be Cousin Cosmo's robot, Tad realized while running his fingers carefully over the surface of the seemingly defunct mechanism. The only one of its kind, the reverend had said. Tad was fairly familiar with the various types of robots and servos manufactured by Rhymer Industries. This slumped giant was nothing that was offered in any of the RI catalogs and brochures.

Straightening, Tad moved back and stood over Electro. "Who did this to you?" he asked. "I guess I'll never find out unless. . . ."

Tad knelt again, felt at the robot's head until he located the concealed skull lock. He applied pressure, there was a mild popping and a small section of the chrome-plated skull swung open.

Turning on his heel, Tad sprinted back to a cabinet where he'd noticed an assortment of lightrods. He had to twist the handles of five before he found one which still gave off light.

Back with Electro, Tad sent the thin beam of light into the opening in the robot's head. "All there, all intact," he said grinning. There had been no damage to the machine's brain, his function center or his memory system. Everything seemed unharmed. "So he could tell me what happened to him. . . . And maybe a lot of other things, too, if. . . . . Yeah, if."

If Tad could fix the enormous robot. If he could repair all the damage done to the control and power center.

Very slowly Tad shut the skull. "I can do it," he said. "Going to take time, a lot of work and patience. But I can make this robot work again."

Chapter 3

Hohl went someplace nights, most nights anyway.

Tad first found that out while ducked behind the row of ugly prickly shrubs which lined the central pathway of the estate. It was a few minutes short of midnight, Tad was long since supposed to have been asleep in his room on the second floor of the mansion. Not tonight, though, because tonight he was going to pay his second visit to the underground lab and begin workings on the damaged robot.

He'd managed to get free of his room, down a back stairway and out into the foggy night undetected. While he was cutting across the damp grass he heard Hohl shouting behind him.

"What kind of hoptoad mount is this, you tin-whistle nerf?" the estate manager was hollering someplace off in the mist.

Tad relaxed some, his breathing coming more regularly. The big man didn't seem to be discussing him.

"Am I supposed to go about my clandestine business on a lop-eared nork of a nag?"

"One is extremely sorry, sir."

That was Biernat, the head butler robot. A headless, tank-shape mechanism.

"Sorry, my dangling booper! This frapping grout is one step from the burger grill! Bring me a better one or I'll put your toke in a sling!"

"One will attempt to do better on one's second try, sir."

"Goodness me, Biernat. Have I been bullyragging you again? Bless me, it's my annoying fog allergy which makes me so cussed all the time. Allow me to take some medication while you fetch a new mount."

"One hastens to fulfill one's mission, sir."

Bong! Kapong!

Biernat fell over onto the walkway. The fog also affected him, making him now and then top-heavy.

"Why don't you watch where you put your frapping feet, you knock-kneed billyweed? I ought. . . . Oops! There I went, ranting again."

"One learns to accept such verbal abuse."

Spang!

Hohl had apparently dealt the metal butler a good-natured par on the back.

"You're a darn good sport, Biernat, putting up with my moods night after night."

Head low, Tad continued on his way through the misty grounds. The voices of Hohl and the robot and the hooffalls of the grout all dimmed and were muffled away into silence.

The multicolored panals of Warehouse 6 loomed suddenly in front of him. Tad let himself in the same side door he'd tampered with to gain entry that afternoon. Some fog creeped in with him, went swirling around the high-stacked crates, the tumbled furniture.

Tad hurried through the cluttered silence and went down into the lab. Using the light rod he'd discovered earlier, he examined the light-strip powerbox. He'd decided he'd allow himself three hours a night down here, with as much additional time as he could snatch safely from each day. His first night all the time went to repairing the lighting system and getting the crisscross strips cleaned.

He did take a moment, before slipping away, to cross to where the giant robot lay slumped. "I'll be getting to you soon," he promised.

The next day he couldn't get underground at all. Biernat seemed nearly always to have an eye on him and when the robot butler wasn't around one of the other mechanical servants was underfoot. Tad decided to attempt to get something out of his forced closeness to the butler.

"Biernat," he asked, when the tank-shape butler served him lunch in the octagonal glaz-walled dining nook, "you've been a servant here for quite awhile, haven't you?"

"One might say that, young sir." He placed a tray on the table.

"In the days when my cousins lived here, I mean."

"Rest their souls," murmured Beirnat, bringing a hand up toward the top of his tank.

Bonk!

"What happened?"

"One asks forgiveness, young sir. One was attempting to wipe away a sentimental tear from one's eye," explained the headless mechanism. "It was not until the fist was in motion that one realized one possesses neither a head nor eye."

"Faulty memory chip," suggested Tad. He picked

up his soysan, didn't bite into it. "I hear there were more servants here in those days."

"Oh, so?"

"In particular there was a robot named. . . . Matter of fact, I don't think I know his name. He was supposed to be a particular favorite of my Cousin Cosmo."

"Electro," said Biernat out of his voice grid. "Many's the time one sat about listening to Electro's pungent comments on the events of. . . . Ah, but one forgets one has been programmed not to discuss Electro. Forgive me, young sir, it must be that very defect of mine you were mentioning which causes me to ramble so."

Tad frowned. "Who told you not to remember Electro?"

The butler shrugged his tank. "One doesn't remember," he answered.

Chapter 4

Anticipation made Tad pace his room in a rapid, bouncing fashion. "Tonight, or tomorrow at the latest," he said aloud. "Yeah, I'll have Electro completely repaired and then . . . then we'll see if he's going to function again."

Tad had become fairly good at dodging Biernat and the various other mechanisms who shared the Foghill mansion with him. Hohl had grown increasingly occupied with whatever business it was he conducted with Reverend Dimchurch. The result was the estate manager had not been on the premises much at all lately. This meant that over the past five weeks, since his discovery of the damaged robot, Tad was able to sneak into the workshop beneath the warehouse with fair frequency. He'd put in a good deal of work on Electro, utilizing the tools left by his late cousin.

He felt he had the robot on the brink of functioning. Tonight, with any luck, he'd bring Electro back to life. "And then I can—"

Rap-a-tap! Rap-a-tap!

As Tad turned toward the thick door of his room it swung open. Monique came rolling in. "You forgot to take your vitamins at dinner, Master Tad."

He scowled at the intruding robot, which was built along the lines of the butler with a series of nozzles attached to its front. "I really don't think I need—"

"We can never pay too much attention to our nutrition," the kitchen staff robot told him. "It's important you have, as a growing boy, your minimum daily requirement of vitamins and minerals as recommended by the Barnum Board of Ag—"

"I'm not growing, Monique. I really think I've ceased growing, attained my full height."

"Ho ho, always kidding, Master Tad." One of the robot's several arms swung up and turned on a chest faucet.

Slurp! Slurp!

"Spoon," advised Tad, watching the vitamin fluid spilling onto his neolin floor.

"To be sure." Another arm brought a spoon under the flowing faucet. When the spoon was filled, the faucet was twisted shut. "Swallow this like a good boy, Master Tad."

He hesitated before slouching forward and allowing the solicitous mechanism to thrust the spoon between his lips. "Okay, thanks," he said swallowing, "and now if—"

"Wouldn't you like a hearty cup of cocosub?"

"Nope, no."

"Neareal egg nog?" Monique tapped the third faucet down on the left side.

"Nothing more, thanks." Reaching out, he gave the robot a polite shove in the direction of the open door.

He faked a yawn. "Tired, ought to hop into bed. Night."

"Sleeping potion?"

"No need."

"I'll say good night, then, Master Tad."

"Splendid, do that."

"Good night." Avoiding the spill of vitamin fluid, Monique wheeled out of the room.

Tad moved to shut the door. The door, however, came swinging back at him.

"Ha! So there you are, you pigeon-toed mammy-jammer!" boomed Hohl as he followed the door into the room.

"Why shouldn't I be here?" Tad took several steps backward. "This is my room."

"Don't go trying any of your beady-eyed logic with me, my lad!" Hohl's thick forefinger jabbed at the narrow corridor of air which separated him from the young man. "All is known!"

"All is known about what?"

The bulky estate manager made a grab, caught hold of Tad's arm. "We'll just march down to the underground lab," he announced in a substantial voice, "and see what kind of monkeyshines you've been up to!"

Chapter 5

Hohl's spell of anger did not subside. He continued to shout and snort while dragging Tad through the mansion, down the broad staircase and out into the night. "Treat you like a frapping prince! Then you go and stick a poniard in my metaphorical—"

"I've been tinkering, that's all." Tad finally managed to wrest free of the bigger man's clutch. "Are you trying to tell me puttering around is some kind of—"

"Enough of your snurly backchat!" Hohl was on the verge of running. "Certain things are forbidden! Putzing around in Cosmo's lab happens to be one of them!"

"Why? There's no possible way I can hurt any—"

"Rule! It's a rule!"

"You should have told me, then."

"Anyone with an ounce of sense would *know* the harping rule!" They'd reached the warehouse and Hohl unlocked the main door.

"I think," said Tad as he followed the estate manager into the darkened dome, "I better get in touch with my Cousin Joshua tomorrow. There's really no reason I can't be allowed to—"

"Joshua! Oh, yeah, sure, certainly. That'll be splendid!" Hohl gave a series of barking laughs. "If he finds out what I've let you get away with, all our norks will be on the block!" His feet thumped loudly on the downward ramp to the lab.

When the lights came on Tad sucked in a deep breath, blinking.

"Who fixed these nerfing fixtures? Did you do that, you snerg-livered little tinker?"

"I did, yes." Tad was watching the far corner of the room.

Electro was back there, back where Tad had first seen him weeks ago. Worse, he was slumped exactly as he had been then. His front hung open, his internal workings dangled. A plump spider was at work decorating his defunct-looking head with thin strands of orange webbing.

Hohl, making sounds somewhere between coughs and hoots, was roaming the workshop. He grabbed up tools, tossed them down. He kicked at tables, poked squat fingers at mechanisms. Gradually he approached the fallen Electro. Standing over the apparently ruined robot, he chuckled in a pleased way. "Looks like I got down here in time, you arrogant piece of scrap!"

Tad leaned against a workbench. Hohl was acting as though he'd not had anything to do with this current wrecking of the robot. Then who had destroyed the five weeks of hard and patient work Tad had put into reviving Electro? Could one of the servants, the one who'd informed on him, have come down here and done this?

"Sir, an urgent summons!" Biernat clattered into the workshop.

"Don't any of you nitbrained goops realize this lab is not to be barged—"

"It's the Reverend Dimchurch, sir," interrupted the butler, arms flapping. "He says the troops may have been alerted about your transactions for this evening!"

"The troops? The norking troops?" Hohl stamped a foot, then went running for the ramp. "They can't do that!"

"Be careful you don't take cold from loitering down here, sir." Biernat followed the estate manager out.

Tad waited a few seconds before rushing to the slumped robot. "Who the hell did this to you, Electro?"

"I did, and you're damn lucky I'm as shrewd as I am." Electro's right arm came up, tucked his workings in and shut the front of him. He scooted the diligent spider away with a swipe of his metal hand. "Never did like spiders trespassing on me. You don't have a metal exterior, but if you did, the tiny *ping-pong* of a spider's tread would drive you goofy."

Tad sat down on his heels all at once. "Who . . . who finished fixing you?"

"Obviously I did. A bright move it was, since you were on the verge of tipping the whole thing to that simp Hohl," replied Electro. He flexed his bright fingers. "I suppose I shouldn't have expected too much from a callow youth, a mere stripling, a dreamy mooncalf who—"

"I'm eighteen, and I knew enough to nearly repair you. In fact, if you hadn't butted in I would have completed you tonight."

"Once I got word that dolt was about to intrude I completed myself," explained Electro. "Next I arranged myself artistically with spider webs and similar muck to create the illusion of long dormancy. Very impressive, wasn't it? Looked a bit like that wedding cake in the Dickens novel. Or does anybody read Dickens in this planet system anymore? Not only did I fool you with my impersonation of a wreck, I—"

"Listen, if I hadn't found you and done most of the work, you'd still be flat on your ass with spiders going *ping-pong* all over you," said Tad, voice rising. "I was told you were a pleasant sort of a machine, but you're turning out to be as big a grouch as Hohl."

"All right, okay, very well. I apologize, I offer my abject regrets." Silently the robot rose up. He was seven feet tall, over a foor higher than his resurrector.

Tad got up, took a few steps away, stood studying the huge machine. "You are Electro, aren't you?"

"Who else would I be? I'm unique, as you'll learn. Full name is Electro-XM13J33. You can call me simply Electro." He rubbed his chrome hands together. "Now, let's be off?"

"Off?"

Electro said, "We have our course laid out for us, my boy. Our path is clear, the road we must follow is—"

"Did my cousin build that tendency toward redundancy into you?"

Electro's blue eyes blinked, making a faint click sound. "I am the proud owner, the sole proprietor, the prime possessor of a vast and thorough vocabulary. In order to make myself crystal clear to any auditor who might not have a mental capacity equal to mine I often—"

"Can you just tell me once what you meant by saying we were off for someplace?"

"Ah, I realize you aren't aware of what's gone before, of the events of the past."

"That's one of the reasons I repaired you. So I

might find out about my cousins and what happened to them."

"Allow me to fill you in." Electro placed a palm on his chest, started pacing back and forth across a distance of about ten feet.

"Why are you strutting like that?"

"This is a well-known declaiming posture."

"I don't want a speech exactly."

The robot was silent and thoughtful for several seconds. "We'll assume another approach." He moved to a stool, sat on it, crossed his legs and rested an elbow on a knee. "An informal posture, suited to man-to-man talk among friends. Better?"

Tad nodded. "What happened here? Why were you ripped open, dumped in the corner?"

"You've touched on one of the saddest experiences of my life," said the robot. "My only excuse is that I was distracted and allowed that lout Hohl to sneak up behind me with a fairly efficient disabler. An RI brand disabler, by the way. He put me on the fritz, had me carted down here and proceeded to use some of these very tools to incapacitate a goodly share of my inner workings. Being a dunce and somewhat preoccupied at the time, he concentrated on my power centers and left my mental facilities alone."

"Was this after Cousin Cosmo was dead?"

Electro said, "Cousin Cosmo isn't dead."

"Huh?" A deep frown touched Tad's face. "What do you mean?"

"I mean quite simply that Cosmo Rhymer is not dead. I've double-checked the fact since I returned to life," said the robot. "Cosmo Rhymer isn't dead, my boy, and neither is your father."

Chapter 6

Tad very slowly reached out to tap the robot's broad chrome chest. "Your brain system is still a little flooey."

"My thinking equipment has never been in a state remotely resembling flooey, my boy," replied Electro. "I assure you, both your father and your Cousin Cosmo are alive at this moment. I hesitate to commit myself to alive and well, since six years at Blackwatch have taken a certain toll. However, once we rescue them the—"

"He's alive? My father is really alive?"

"That's the news I'm trying to convey. I'd heard you were a relatively bright youth but this—"

"But he's supposed to be dead. They told us that, gave us a little box of ashes."

"Most ashes look alike. You and your mother were flummoxed, flimflammed and hoaxed."

"I don't understand. Why?"

"If you'll cease interrupting my discourse you'll eventually understand the true circumstances."

"Okay, all right, tell me. And what's Blackwatch?"

"Blackwatch doesn't come into the narrative until later, my boy. Allow me to observe the dramatic unities, which were first set down in the Solar System by a moderately gifted fellow name of Arist—"

"My father, it's him I want to hear about."

Electro tilted his head slightly to the left. "You'll need some background details. To begin with, your Cousin Joshua is a crook and scoundrel."

"I figured as much. Did he put my father in Blackwatch, whatever that is?"

"As I was saying, your Cousin Joshua and your Cousin Cornelia had been up to no good, fleecing Rhymer Industries in a variety of ways for nearly a year before Cosmo, alerted by a rather gross and slow-witted computer, got wise. Had he relied on me, the schemes and machinations of Joshua would have come to light much earlier. That is, alas, neither here nor there," said Electro. "Before Cosmo could act or confront his criminous cousin, Joshua found out the jig was well nigh up. He descended on Foghill with a large band of goons and, I ruefully admit, defeated us. The bombastic Hohl was among that initial set of goons and it was he, as I've mentioned, who disabled me and mutilated my person." The big robot's head dropped, metal chin clicking against metal chest.

"And my father?"

"Cosmo had, very cautiously, summoned your father here to Esmeralda to inform him of what he'd unearthed about Joshua," explained the robot. "Before your father even reached Foghill he was intercepted by yet another batch of goons. Then your father and Cosmo were conveyed across the planet to the Blackwatch Plantation. It's a wretched place, more penal colony than agricultural facility, secretly owned and operated by Joshua. To think that man is over one-half machine. Well, blood will tell."

"Why didn't he simply kill them, my father and Cousin Cosmo and his wife?"

"Joshua apparently possesses a small sentimental streak, which prevents him from killing near relatives. Robots belonging to near relatives, as we've seen, he has no such qualms about."

"Is Cousin Alice on the plantation, too?"

"In some sort of menial culinary capacity, yes."

"They've been there six years," said Tad. "Six years while we thought they were dead and my mother died still thinking. . . ."

Electro put a metal arm around the young man's shoulders. "It's an imperfect world, Tad, even with such highly efficient mechanisms as myself in it," he said. "It's been very frustrating for me, over these six years, lying here with my brain gathering all these dreadful facts about people I care for and being unable to do anything much in the way of helping them. But now we can take action at last."

"Yes, right." Tad moved free of him. "We've got to contact the police, tell them what—"

"Fat chance," cut in the robot. "Your Cousin Joshua, now that he's head of RI, had considerable influence with the local, national and international police-keeping bodies on this planet. You go to them and the odds are you'll be the one who ends up in the jug."

"But that's rotten."

"This is an imperfect world, to repeat myself."

"Okay, then we have to get to this plantation as fast as we can. We'll get hold of some kind of skycar to—"

"Whoa, halt. We can't be anywhere near that direct," said Electro. "Once we take our leave of Foghill, my boy, Joshua will loose a pack of his goons on our trail. If we avail ourselves of any of the obvious means of transport we'll be picked off like that."

Ping!

Electro'd snapped his metal fingers.

"We have to travel some less obvious way, then," said Tad. "But how?"

"Leave that to my vaunted ingenuity."

"Whoever vaunted your ingenuity?"

"They well would have, had I not been languishing here," replied the robot. "I really am an exceptional person . . . exceptional product if you prefer. We'll leave shortly, taking advantage of the fact Hohl and his cronies are down by the river."

"What river?"

"The River Sneath. You'd best impress the name on your brain, since we'll likely be using the Sneath on part of our journey."

"How far away is Blackwatch?"

"Nearly five hundred miles." With a barely a creak, the giant robot went striding toward the exit.

"What exactly is Hohl up to? Do you know?"

"Of course I know. Even before I returned to the living I was able to reconnoiter and—"

"How do you do that while sitting down here covered with cobwebs?"

"You are a bit flippant, exactly as predicted in your dossier," said Electro over his bright shoulder. "My boy, with my searching mind I can contact computers, databanks, robots and androids and sundry other mechanisms in the vicinity and beyond. The result is facts pouring into my ample brain." He shook his head briefly. "Unfortunately, while I was somewhat defunct, my searching mind worked at nowhere near capacity. But now . . . Ah!"

"So what exactly is Hohl up to?"

"He's a smuggler." The robot beckoned. "Let us travel upwards."

"Does that mean Reverend Dimchurch is a smuggler as well?"

"It does indeed, yes."

"He seemed to me like. . . . I don't know, an honest man."

"Many smugglers are." They emerged on a foggy stretch of grass. Electro made inhaling sounds, tapping his chest. "The great outdoors and pure unprocessed air."

"Do you have lungs?"

"I have all sorts of handy attachments. I can even play alto saxophone." Electro nodded in the direction of the mansion, which was barely visible in the thick mist. "We'll pack before commencing on our jour—"

"I don't want to waste time. I'll travel with what I have on my back."

"An admirable and symbolic gesture, but screwy in this instance," Electro told him. "You'll need warmer clothes for some of the country we have to cross. We also need cash."

"Clothes I have, but hardly any money."

"Hohl has wads of it in his safe."

"Can you open his safe?"

"There are, my boy, very few things I can't do," answered Electro. "When we have more time I'll run you off a complete list."

Chapter 7

Two men materialized, furtively carrying a microwave robot chef. They grunted and muttered and were eaten up by the thick fog.

Electro swung out a cautionary hand. "Halt a moment, lad," he advised in a whisper. "We appear to be in the midst of the smugglers."

Tad pressed against the bole of a huge dark tree, flattening his backpack somewhat. "What do you think Hohl will do if he—"

"Try to disable me and lock you up." Electro shook his head, which was faintly beaded with mist. "We don't want that to happen. Come along, we'll shift to a Southerly direction for a spell."

They encountered only silence and fog for the next several minutes.

"Congratulations! You've won two more free games of Worlds Collide!" boomed out a tinny voice.

"Hush it up, cobber!"

"How the blinking hell can I? It's got a flapping mind of its own, cobber."

"Yes, because you achieved the incredible score of 46,000 points you win two more fun-filled and excitement-packed games of Worlds Collide, the interplanetary destruction game which is fun for the whole family, parental discretion advised!"

"Kick the blinking thing!"

"I did and busted me flapping paw."

"Well, drop it, then, and let's whack it with a bleeding rock!"

"Worlds Collide, the dynamic game which teaches you cosmology while you have fun!"

"Next time we lug a servo and not one of these blinking recmecs."

Tad and Electro had stopped still at the first noise. Two of the smugglers, nearby but completely hidden by the swirling fog, were having trouble with a malfunctioning game machine.

"Step right up, step right up! Play Worlds Collide!"

"Hush, hush, won't you?"

"Step on it, jump on it!"

"Oh, yes, and then bust it. Wouldn't Hohl love that."

"He ain't going to fancy all this bleeding hooroar, cobber."

"What is all this bleeding hooroar about!" screamed a new voice.

"Hohl," whispered Tad.

"We was just talking about you, Hohl. Seems this flapping machine got bunged up whilst we was hefting it off the barge during our recent clandestine nocturnal activities and now it's taken to shooting off its ruddy—"

"I'll shoot off your ruddy snout if you don't silence it!" shouted the unseen estate manager.

"Let's push onward while they're squabbling," suggested Electro as he took hold of Tad's arm.

Tad hesitated. "I'd like to get a last look at Hohl," he said. "Tell him how I've felt about all the—"

"We don't have time for settling scores right now," the robot reminded. "Later, perhaps." He tugged.

"Okay, we'll go. But . . ."

In a few moments they were out of range of the squabble. All was fog and silence again.

Until they tramped into a clearing in the mist and saw a circle of a dozen men. Catmen, lizard men, humans. Some carried illegal machines, but some carried blaster rifles and stunguns.

"What have we here?" muttered a thickset catman. He held a blaster pistol in his left paw. "A wee lad and his 'bot nanny, is it?"

"On the contrary," said Electro while glancing from weapon to weapon, "we're part of the mob."

"The what?"

"The mob, the gang, the bunch," amplified the robot. "We work for Hohl, same as you."

"We ain't got any 'bots on the team," pointed out a stooped lizard man. "We smuggle 'bots, we don't work with 'em."

"No, we don't rub shoulders and socialize with 'bots," added the catman with the pistol.

"He's an expensive-looking model," said the lizard man, circling Electro. "Fetch a good price in the capital, wouldn't he now?"

"He happens to be mine," said Tad, his voice a shade unsteady. "And I happen to be Hohl's boss . . . you might say I'm the mastermind behind this entire operation. So you guys had—"

"Ha!" laughed the catman, scratching at his furry flickering ear with the tip of the blaster barrel. "A mooncalf claiming to be the mastermind what bosses Hohl."

"I'm tired of being called a mooncalf!" Tad took two steps forward.

Electro caught him. "Diplomacy is what's called for, my boy," he said in a low voice. "Allow me to negotiate with these rogues and rascals. Now then, sir, if you'll—"

"By the blessed bones of St. Serpentine! What's going on?" The Reverend Dimchurch came rolling out of the surrounding fog in his cart.

"Reverend Dimchurch," said Tad.

The lizard priest brought his purple scarf up and dabbed at his dry lips. "I had hoped, and occasionally prayed, Tad, you'd never encounter me in this context," he said sadly. "However, as St. Reptillicus reminds us in his 27th Epistle to the Greengrocer, 'Some nights you can't get a drink on the cuff anyplace.' "

"You know this mooncalf?" asked the catman.

"He's a close friend of mine." The reverend's eyes widened, then focused on Electro. "And this formidable metallic creation can be none other than—"

"Incognito," rushed in Electro. "I'd prefer to travel incognito."

"Ah, yes. I see." And where exactly are you traveling to, you and Tad?"

Tad replied, "I'm leaving Foghill. I can't explain why just now, though possibly you know."

"We all must wander some in our youth. Doesn't St. Reptillicus, in his oft-quoted 19th Epistle to the Furniture Company, tell us, 'If they won't deliver, you've got to go out for the stuff'?" He made a mystical sign in the misty air. "May St. Serpentine be with you on your journey, no matter what its duration or ultimate destination."

"Thanks, reverend," said Tad.

The catman snarled. You mean to let them go, rev?"

"They are to continue unmolested, and no mention made of this incident to Hohl?"

"How come?" demanded the angry smuggler. "How come, rev?"

The lizard priest's eyes rolled skyward. "It is the will of God, my friends."

"Okay," said the catman, "we won't argue with that."

Electro got hold of Tad's arm again. "We'll be on our way once more," he told the group, moving away from them with Tad in tow. "Pleasant running into you again after all these years, reverend."

"Yes, yes," said Dimchurch, waving a green hand. "Don't forget the advice of St. Reptillicus. 'Some towns have hardly any saloons at all.' Good-bye."

Soon Tad and the robot were alone again, moving toward the river.

Chapter 8

Electro gestured with one glistening metal hand. "Below us lies Fetid Landing."

"They're very literal with names hereabouts." Tad halted beside the robot at the edge of the forest and looked down across the misty night hillside. "Fetid Landing, Foghill."

"What can you expect from people with organic brains?" He swung his arm leftwards, caught the back of Tad's tunic as the young man was about to start downhill for the tumbledown river town.

"Now what?"

"Now, stripling, we must avail ourselves of more of my built-in cunning."

"You haven't been especially cunning so far, Electro. You let us walk right smack into that band of smugglers. Then we didn't even try to fight our way out."

"Wisdom comes either with years or superior technology," the robot told him. "Trust me, therefore, until you develope sufficient wisdom of your own. Before we enter even a shabby town like Fetid Landing we must disguise ourselves."

Tad said, "You actually think Cousin Joshua will come hunting us?"

"Joshua, Hohl, Cornelia and a multitude of goons," Electro assured him. "After all, I know far too much and you are the rightful heir to the entire Rhymer Industries empire. We're lucky Hohl is too preoccupied with his smuggling to have noticed our departure yet."

"Wait. Am I the heir? I didn't know that."

"Naturally, since they didn't want you to know."

"But my mother would have kno—"

"She was flummoxed, same as you and your slack-witted attorney. But enough babbly on the subject of familial crookedness." He fisted his left side, causing a small door to pop open.

"I never noticed that when I was repairing you."

"See my earlier reference to wisdom." From the opening Electro withdrew an oblong box marked DISGUISE KIT. "I happen to be a makeup wizard." He delved into the kit, extracting a tube of something green. "While I'm doing this, reach into your rucksack, my boy, for that cloak I foresightedly snatched out of the wardrobe closet. No use greening up my entire body."

"You're going to paint yourself green?" Tad slung off his knapsack, dug around until he located the plaid cloak.

"I am converting myself into a lizard man."

Draping the cloak over a tree branch, Tad remarked, "This particular plaid won't go with green."

"A gentleman of style can wear anything. I set trends, lad, I don't follow them."

"For somebody who usually goes around unclothed you claim—"

"My brain is a storehouse of fashion lore. Here, hold this mirror while I produce the scale effect."

Tad held the small oval at eye level. "You sure you can be a convincing lizard man?"

Electro stooped slightly, went about creating scales on the green substance he'd applied to his chrome face. "What does it take to be a lizard? One of the dullest types in the known universe. Snooze in the sun, catch flies with your tongue, shed your skin now and then."

"Reverend Dimchurch was much more versatile than—"

"Oh, right, he was also a smuggler." Electro paused to inspect his progress. "Seems fairly convincing in this rather mucky moonlight. What do you think?"

"Yep, you're starting to look like a lizard."

"When we encounter anyone I'll not only look like a lizard man, I'll act like one."

"Cousin Cosmo built an awful lot of talents into you."

"Yes," agreed Electro, wagging his now lizard-like head. "I'll do the hands next, possibly the arms up to the elbows. Then we'll tackle you."

Tad protested, "You're not going to turn me into a lizard."

"You couldn't bring it off," said Electro. "All we need do with you is lighten your hair and give you a smattering of beard. Joshua's scouts will be seeking news of a dark lad and an imposing robot. They'll ignore gossip and rumors about a blond young fellow traveling with an overweight lizard man."

"I suppose so."

"You don't sound terrifically confident." The robot applied artificial lizard skin to his metal hands.

"It's only that, well, Electro, you've been in that underground lab for six years," said Tad. "Out here the world is different, this theatrical bluffing may not work."

"You haven't led that worldly a life yourself so far. At least according to your dossier."

"I lived at home, went to a fairly private school, didn't travel much," Tad admitted. "There never seemed to be enough money for anything beyond the essentials. My mother kept me close to her, maybe because she didn't want any accidents to happen to me."

"Very well then," said the robot. "We're both in need of practical experience. Let us, therefore, proceed to gather some."

"First we better change the color of my hair," said Tad.

Chapter 9

The building hung out over the dark waters of the river, supported by bowlegged stilts. It was pocked with round windows of multicolored glaz, had roofs of slanting slate. The large wooden sign over the doorway proclaimed it as the Belles Lettres Cafe & Boarding House. Noise, smoke and harsh fumes were spilling out of the open window ovals. And as Tad and Electro approached the entrance the double doors popped open to allow two husky catmen waiters to heave a protesting owlman out into the foggy night.

"We don't go for no fanatic existential humanists in here, bud!" growled one of the waiters while the flung owlman was rolling over on the slippery flagstones.

"Perhaps I didn't make myself clear," said the moderately intoxicated customer. "My stand is not the traditional philosophic pose of—"

"Ar, stuff it in your feathery nork, mate!" suggested the other waiter, making a threatening gesture with one fisted paw.

His associate was eyeing Tad. "You ain't planning to start some kind of tasteless debate, are you?"

"Not at all, sir," answered Electro for him. "We merely seek shelter and a warm meal."

The waiter grunted, stood aside so they might enter. "Go on in, cobbers, but keep your blinking noses clean," he advised. "Don't refute the boss too much, he's in a fair foul mood this blinking night."

"We appreciate your advice," said Electro, urging Tad into the crowded main room of the cafe.

"This seems like a place where we're going to get trouble, not help." Tad stood surveying the blurred room.

There were fifteen or so round tables on the raw wood floor. The light, dim and fuzzy, came from floating amber globes up near the low, beamed ceiling. A bar covered one wall and standing behind it, swaying from left to right, was a lanky lizard man in the purple robes of a bishop of the Church of Aggressive Beatitude.

"The wavering gent would be the proprietor," explained Electro out of the side of his now-green mouth. "Defrocked cleric who calls himself Bish. Fancies himself a man of letters, hence the name of this bistro and the frequent philosophical and literary skirmishes which take place herein."

"See anyone who can help us?" Tad moved toward a vacant table.

"As I mentioned previously," said the disguised robot, "your cousin used to allow me to accompany him to Fetid Landing now and again. Thus I came to know some of his local friends. If I can contact certain of them I'll be able to arrange passage out for us. Otherwise, we'll take potluck and approach the least rascally appearing riverman."

"Over here, you two promising-looking chaps."

Bish was flapping a green inviting hand at them from behind the bar.

"We'd prefer a table if you—"

"Boss wants a friendly discourse with you two blokes." Another large waiter, human this one, appeared at Electro's side. "Don't antagonize him."

"We've been traveling a full weary day," said the robot. "Couldn't we dine and—"

"Discourse first, then food." The waiter hustled them up to the bar.

Bish gave a pleased chuckled when he noticed their arrival. "Two coves of obvious intellect," he said. "Clearly several cuts above the usual run of dimwits we get at the Belles Lettres. Take that owlish gent who just received the old heave, he didn't know his blip from a snerg hole. And him claiming to be a professor at the University of California on Jupiter. Not bloody likely. What'll it be, lads?"

"What sort of ale do you have?" asked Electro, leaning an elbow on the bar and producing, at least to Tad's ears, a metallic thunk.

"No, no, I don't mean what blinking kind of swill you want to slosh into your blooming gullet." Bish's gaunt green left hand jabbed out, pointing at a large blackboard propped against the liquor shelves behind him. "What intellectual topic do you wish to discuss?"

Today's Special was chalked across the top of the blackboard in a mismatched style of lettering. Below was a scrawled list.

1. *Chromatic Aberration*
2. *Kepler's Second Law*
3. *Megavitamin Therapy*
4. *Harlan Ellison's Green Period*
5. *The Later Miracles of St. Reptillicus*

Electro stroke his chin with his scaly knuckle. "Rather sparse fare tonight, Bish."

"We had to scratch a couple of topics," said the one-time bishop. "Too controversial, they was. In fact, number seven provoked three brawls, a broken marriage and a scimitar-knifing between sunset and about a half hour ago. I won't even tell you what that particular topic was, lest you be moved to violence. How about taking Kepler? I'm always good for twenty minutes of heated interchange about that old sod."

Electro rested his other elbow on the bar top, making a lesser thunk. "I was hoping to discuss transportation," he confided. "More specifically, transportation along the River Sneath."

Bish made a rude sound. "That's no fit subject for men of intellect to chew the blinking rag over."

"It is, nonetheless, a topic I will pay a small but impressive sum to discuss," continued the robot. "Earlier inquiries have led me to believe that a few rivermen I knew in former times still travel the Sneath. Should I be able to contact one of them this night, I'd be very pleased."

"Ar, you're just offering a little cumshaw to me for setting up an interview 'twixt you and one of these sods who run boats on the river," said Bish. "Hardly the sort of exchange I anticipated when you entered, mates." He swayed in Tad's direction. "Are you as intellectually sterile as this verdant pritz here, young fellow?"

"If we chat a few minutes about Kepler, will you help us locate the people we want?"

"Now here's a true intellectual," said Bish, attempting to reach across the bar to par Tad's shoulder. Instead he slipped, tumbling head foremost into an ice bin behind the bar.

Tad said to the robot, "Maybe there's an easier way to contact this Commodore Snow or the other riverboat people you mentioned."

"This place is the crossroads of Fetid Landing, the favored hangout of rivermen," replied Electro. "If Snow is in town, he'll be somewhere in this vicinity. Perhaps in a private room above. Same goes for Skipper Anmar, Harpoon Louie and One-Eye Reisberson."

"Where was I?" Bish, upright again, inserted his little finger into an ear hole to grind out a few flecks of cracked ice.

"Kepler," said Tad.

"Ah, yes, Kepler, the astronomical sod. Let us begin by analyzing his cockeyed notions about—"

Slam!

Bam!

Crash!

Three people had come tromping and shoving into the cafe, accompanied by a battered and mean-spirited robot. Two of the newcomers were lizard men, red skinned, and the other was an albino catman. The robot had once been painted an eggshell white, but was now much chipped and dirt smeared. Wisps of steam drifted out of his battered ears.

"Trouble," muttered Bish. "Whenever you get more than one red liz in a room, you've got trouble coming."

"All righty," boomed one of the red lizard men, "where's the pussy?"

Bish swallowed, tried to slow his swaying. "Gents, this is a blinking, eating, lodging and debating sort of establishment," he called out to them. "If you seek—"

"Stow that dilettante crap," advised the other red lizard. "We come for the pussy."

"I might suggest you fellows try the Temps Perdu Hotel over on Red Snapper Lane across—"

"We don't want to *buy* pussy," said the catman, his

pink eyes narrowed. "We come to fetch home the pussy you're hiding here!"

Bish gathered his purple robes tighter around his lean body. "Am I to understand you are alluding to one of my boarders?"

"That's right, the blonde pussy," said a red lizard.

"Hand her over to us and we'll drag her home to her goddamn lawful husband," said the other lizard man. "No trouble for you, no questions asked."

"That, my friends, would be a violation of the young woman's basic civil rights," began Bish. "Something I simply can not—"

"Ambrose, persuade this bugger!" The catman nudged the robot.

A few scabs of white paint fell from the mechanism as he lumbered closer to the bar. "Give us . . . the pussy," he said in a rumbling, rattling voice. "Else I . . . use me fingers . . . on you, sumbitch!"

"This lout's in dreadful shape," said Electro quietly to Tad. "A victim of very slipshod maintenance."

Tad said, "These guys came here to drag away some girl against her will. We can't—"

"We have to step aside and let them go about their business," said Electro.

"But it *is* a violation of her civil—"

"We don't know the circumstances or the issues involved. Therefore our best course of action is to ig—"

Zzitz!

Zizzle!

Zam!

Ambrose, the delapidated robot, had aimed three of his metal fingers at the proprietor. From each in turn he spurted a beam of different colored light.

The first had caused Bish to stiffen, the second made him howl and shut his eyes, the third sent him falling to the floor.

"Waiter, come here!" one of the red lizards ordered a catman waiter. "You know where the blonde pussy's room is! Take us!"

"Really, mate, I'm as ignorant as a newborn quilp as to—"

"Ambrose!"

"A moment now, cobber. It occurs to me you must be seeking the lass in room 26B. I'll give you a key. I'll show you how to get up there. I'll fix you a snack from the sandwich board."

"Get the key," the catman instructed Ambrose.

"Key . . . gimme." The battered robot tottered in the direction of the fearful waiter.

The rest of the customers in that area of the cafe moved rapidly back.

"A disgrace to the profession," said Electro, frowning at the actions of Ambrose.

"Listen, Electro, we can't let these guys do this," insisted Tad. "I mean, break in here, stun the owner, drag off the girl. It's simply not—"

"We don't want to attract attention to ourselves," reminded Electro. "Otherwise we may never get out of town. Our first loyalty is to your father and your cousins. We can't afford to—"

"I know that. But this is wrong, and we have to stop it."

Electro shook his green hand. "Forget it, ignore it," he said. "We're not going to risk our safety for some unknown runaway wife whose husband is probably fully justified in having her forceably carted back to his hearthside." The robot moved a hand toward Tad's arm.

Tad pushed him away, spun. "I'm going to do something!" He ran, dived at the back of the nearest red lizard man.

Chapter 10

Hardly turning, almost indifferently, the red lizard man swing back his fist. "Not smart, kid."

The hard scaly fist smacked into Tad's jaw, jolting his head back and causing him to shut his mouth with a grinding snap. One knee slapped the floor; he teetered.

"Not smart at all." The lizard man followed with a chop to the neck.

Tad cried out, biting air. His cheek was all at once hitting the raw wood planking of the cafe floor.

Zzip!

What was that? Was it that beat-up robot again?

The floor seemed to hold him like a magnet held a chunk of iron. Tad struggled, pushed with both hands flat out, finally succeeded in rising to his knees.

The lizard man was directly above him, one hand raised.

Tad flinched, before he realized the red lizard was frozen in his position.

"Most extraordinary," Bish, conscious and upright again, was saying to Electro. "One rarely encounters a fellow lizard with such powers. By the sacred and allegedly sacred bones of St. Giganticus, that was quite a thing to do with just one finger."

"I have a touch of mystical powers." To the three remaining intruders he said, "I won't have anyone hurting my young companion. You'd best beat a hasty retreat."

"Flog yourself," snarled the unfrozen red lizard man. "No bloke can stun my lifelong chum and get off with it!"

Tad concentrated on his breathing for the next several seconds. On that and the tiny dots of intense yellow light which were, ever more slowly, dancing across his field of vision.

"I fix . . . him . . . real good." Ambrose came thudding at Electro.

Zzizz!

Electro had cocked his thumb at the rundown robot. A sizzling line of scarlet brightness leaped out and found the dead center of Ambrose's jigsaw chest.

Ambrose commenced folding, knee joints first, then elbows. In under a minute he was slumped on the floor near Tad.

"Impressive, highly impressive," commented Bish. "Could you teach me how to—"

"It's genetic." Electro, right hand still raised, was staring at the red lizard and the albino catman. "Let me once again suggest your departure."

"We come for the blonde pussy," said the catman. "We don't go without her."

"You going to get into a lot of trouble," warned the red lizard, "messing in our affairs."

"I whole-heartedly agree," said Electro. "However—"

From elsewhere in the building had come the cry of a girl in pain.

Tad was getting to his feet. "Upstairs someplace," he said.

"We got a bigger gang than what you see here," said the catman, laughing and purring.

"They're abducting the young woman," said Bish.

"Electro," shouted Tad, "we have to help her."

"I really feel it wiser, my boy, to—"

"Come on."

"Very well, but first . . ." Rays emanated from the robot's ring and middle fingers.

The red lizard man fell down, the catman froze where he stood.

"Where's 26B?" Tad asked the bishop.

"Out that door yonder, stairs on your left, second landing and to your right."

Tad began to run.

Electro followed.

Up above them somewhere the girl cried out again.

"By the way," said Electro while they bounded up the narrow wooden staircase, "it doesn't help my disguise any when you blurt out my true name in public places, my boy."

"Did I? I didn't realize. Sorry."

"Joshua's goons will have an easier time tracking us if you continue to hoot and holler my rather uncommon name about."

Tad took the next flight of steps two and three at a time.

Then he saw the girl.

She was slender, blonde—older than he was, but not by more than two or three years. She was wearing a short-skirted tunic dress and one of the lizard men struggling with her had a paw up under it.

"I'll hurt you more," he said, "if you don't quit fighting."

There were three more up in the shadowy hallway beneath the floating amber globe of light. Two ragtag catmen and a husky robot in nearly as bad shape as Ambrose of downstairs. One of the catmen had a coil of rope slung over his shaggy arm, the other held a large rough-spun sack.

"Let go of her," said Tad.

The nearest catman dropped his rope, drew out a gun and fired it directly at him.

Chapter 11

Music and sunlight began intruding.

The music was loud and brassy, the sunlight pale and thin. And he was rocking gently, flat on his back.

There was the girl again. Sitting, hands folded, her slim figure haloed by the pale light of early morning which was coming in at the round bobbing window.

The source of the music wasn't in the cabin. It was outside somewhere.

The blonde girl was smiling, tentatively, down at him.

He rocked back with his elbows, pushing himself into a nearly sitting position on the wall bunk. "We're not," he said, his voice dry and strange, "at the inn."

The girl nodded. She was very pretty, he noticed. Something he hadn't been fully aware of when he'd first seen her at the Belles Lettres last . . . had it been last night?

"I've been unconscious for awhile," he said.

"Yes."

"How long, do you know?"

"About ten hours."

"He used a stungun on me, then, nothing deadly."

"They were instructed not to kill anyone, I believe."

Tad sat up suddenly straighter. "Hey, do they have us?"

"No." She smiled again, very cautiously. "We're aboard a riverboat."

"Electro got us out of there?"

"Your companion, yes. He took care of the whole crew of them." She was watching her folded hands.

Tad relaxed, became aware again of the music from the deck above. "What's the music for?"

"A rehearsal I think. This is a showboat."

Tad ran his tongue over his dry lips. "How long have you been sitting here?"

"Most of the night."

"You should have rested."

"I feel responsible."

"No, you didn't force me to barge in."

"Even so."

He flexed his fingers, rubbed at his forehead, stretched. "Electro brought us to this boat, after we got away from the inn?"

"He brought you here," she replied. "I tagged along. He wasn't pleased."

"Electro hasn't had much experience in the world," Tad explained. "You'll have to excuse him."

Her smile widened. "The both of you plucked me out of a nasty setup."

"It was mostly Electro's doing. Since I was out cold for most of it."

The girl left the chair, crossed to the sun-bright porthole. "I'd better tell you a few things," she said. "My name is Jana Taine. I'm twenty-four years old and—"

"Twenty-four? I thought you were younger. Oh, excuse me."

She asked, "You're nineteen or twenty?"

"Nearly."

"That's why twenty-four seems old to you." She was staring out at the river. "I've been married for two and a half years to a man named Rodlow Taine. He's thirty-five. He manages the Rhymer Industries Household Servo plant in—"

"Rhymer Industries?"

"He's quite important to them, to RI." She turned to watch him. "Why does the—"

"I'm a Rhymer. Tad Rhymer."

"Oh," said Jana. She pressed back against the cabin wall.

"Right now, I'm an outcast Rhymer," he said quickly. "I mean, I won't turn you in or call up RI or anything. We're on the run from my Cousin Joshua."

"That would be Joshua Rhymer?"

"Do you know him?"

"Oh, yes. Rodlow's a protégé of his," said the girl. "And he's responsible, your cousin, for my father being where he is."

Tad swung a leg over the bunk edge. "Wait now, did Joshua do something to your father? Put him someplace?"

"It's called Blackwatch Plantation."

Tad was on his feet. "But that's where my father was taken," he told her. "Electro and I are. . . ." The floor was starting to teeter-totter. His stomach filled with hollow pain.

Jana ran to him, slipped an arm around him. "Better sit again, Tad," she advised. "Takes quite awhile to get over a stungun jolt. I know."

She was warm against him. He found he had difficulty swallowing. "I'm okay," he said. "Not used to being on a boat is all."

The girl guided him to the bunk, made him sit. Before she moved away Jana leaned and kissed him on the cheek. "I'm impressed with you already, Tad," she said quietly. "You don't have to lie to me. It's no great shame to be woozy after something like what happened to you."

He didn't exactly catch all the words. He said finally, "I do feel . . . well, unsteady."

"I'm impulsive sometimes," Jana said, returning to the porthole. "Don't let the fact that a married lady of twenty-four kissed you out of appreciation unsettle you. Things like that will happen to you from now on, usually meaning not much."

"Not much," he echoed. "Did you tell Electro about yourself?"

"Some. Enough to make him think, I'm afraid, that I'm not the sort of cargo you should take along on this trip."

"But if your father is being held at Blackwatch, then we ought to work together," said Tad. "We're going to get my father free and clear of that place. Him and my two cousins, all dumped there by Joshua. You were going to try getting your dad out, weren't you?"

Jana asked, "You're offplanet?"

"From Barnum, yes."

"This planet isn't quite as civilized as yours. A man like Joshua Rhymer can pretty well do what he wants," Jana said. "I'll be honest with you, Tad, my main reason for running this time was to get away from my husband. I want to see my father away from Blackwatch, but I really didn't have any kind of plan." She clenched her fists, paced along the cabin wall. "There's one other thing I'd better tell you, so you'll have a better idea of the kind of person I am."

Tad sat watching her. "What?"

"I didn't go to that ramshackle Belles Lettres alone," she said. "I was with someone, a man."

Tad frowned. "We didn't see—"

"He left. Awhile before the trouble started," Jana said. "He did help me get clear of Rodlow, I'll give him that. Then he must have realized I wasn't worth the risk. Usually they do. So if you're considering helping me out, be prepared to come to similar conclusion eventually."

"I'm going to help you," he said. "There's no limit on it. We'll get your father away from Blackwatch. So you don't have to—"

"Up and around at long last? Good." Electro came thumping into the cabin. He had shed his lizard man disguise, was his gleaming chrome self again. "Perhaps, now your vigil is over, Mrs. Taine, you ought to get some rest."

"A splendid idea. See you, Tad." Very quickly she left them.

Tad said, "I'm wondering if Cousin Cosmo didn't build too much rudeness in you."

"You resent people calling you a mooncalf, yet you persist in behaving like one." Electro tapped a metal finger on a metal palm. "Don't go getting sentimental about that young woman. I made a few discreet inquiries after I took care of her husband's goons. Her reputation around the Belles Lettres was—"

"We're going to help her."

Electro gave a majestic shrug. "I'm just another Rhymer servo, thus I must do as bidden," he said. "However, I feel compelled to point out that—"

"Don't," Tad advised. "Instead tell me whose boat we're aboard."

"I located Commodore Snow shortly after our tussle," explained the robot. "Seems the old cat gentleman was having a little assignation and a full course dinner in a room near that of your Mrs. Taine. You don't associate vegetarians, which the commodore is, with intimate late suppers and bouts of gluttony, but that's what he was up to. I was able to arrange, since he's an old friend of Cosmo's, a satisfactory deal for passage. Though he wouldn't throw in Mrs. Taine's fare for nothing and therefore we're out an extra—"

"What are they rehearsing on deck?"

"This evening's performance. We're due to dock at Siltville at sundown. First show an hour later."

"I'll go up and watch."

"You ought to have some breakfast," said Electro. "Commodore Snow maintains a good galley, for a vegetarian. They tell me the carrot flapjacks are—"

"Not especially hungry." Tad, his step still a trifle unsteady, made his way to the door.

"My boy," said Electro toward his back.

"Yeah?"

"Our recent adventure at the Belles Lettres did not aid our cause," said the robot. "I was forced to tip my hand, to reveal my true nature, to utilize powers few lizard men possess. Mrs. Taine's husband is probably as determined a tracker as your Cousin Joshua. We have to be extremely cautious from now on."

"You don't have to worry about me." Tad left the cabin.

Chapter 12

There was still a faint mist hanging over the broad river. The huge paddle wheel of the showboat chopped at the water, the bright forest drifted swiftly by.

A cyborg came along the deck, thrust out his hand. "Hope my music didn't wake you."

"No," said Tad. "The effects of the stungun wore off and—"

Tweet!

When he shook hands a wheezing whistling sound came out of the cyborg's metal elbow.

"Excuse that, excuse it. Forgot to turn myself completely off. My first three wives were all the time complaining about that. Fourth one was tone deaf so she never . . . I'm Washboard Will, the One Man Band. You probably have some of my records in your collection."

"I don't believe so, no."

Washboard Will was a lanky man, a combination

of flesh and metal. His head was topped with a silver skull cap from which several whistle-like tubes extended. There was a row of dials and buttons built into his partially exposed flesh chest. "Sold over ten million albums in the Barnum System alone. And down in the Solar System. . . . Ever hear of that one? Down there, on a planet they call Jupiter, they have a Washboard Will Fan Club, with seventeen chapters. Idolize me on Jupiter."

Pooty Poot!

"Did that come out of your ear?"

"Excuse me, excuse it." Will reached up his metal hand to turn off his ear. "Built most of this equipment myself. Little things will go on the fritz. Drove my first three spouses to distraction. One would hug me, out would come a military march. A kiss on the cheek might produce a rousing polka. Once in bed with, the second one as I recall, a mere playful twist of my . . . but you're probably not interested in my domestic troubles. Had breakfast?"

"Not really very hungry, thanks." Tad glanced around the deck. Up forward was a stage and rows of seats. A striped canopy of blue and gold sheltered the stage and audience area. At the moment the seats were empty, an orange-toned man with four arms was juggling a variety of small furniture. "Was that you I heard playing earlier?"

"None other," replied Will. "There's only one Washboard Will, and his sound is unmistakable. See, unlike some of your one-man-band acts, I have a big-band sound. Sure, because I made all the modifications of myself. I remember vividly the morning I was hacking off my left arm so I could replace it with—"

"You mean this isn't because of an accident?"

"Accident? Since when did great art result from an

accident?" Will shook his head, the whistles built into his skull swayed. "My first wife was the same way as you. When she chanced to notice me whacking off the arm she let out an awful howl. And later, when I bestowed a friendly pat on the toke, she screamed like a stuck quilp. How many women, in their entire lives, get their fannies fondled by a hand that can make as beautiful music as this one?" He held it up, let the sun catch it. "Well, I'm off to the galley. Sure you won't join me?"

"Not right now, thanks." Tad continued along the deck, one hand resting on the railing. They were traveling through an uninhabited area, there was only thick forest on both sides of them.

"Don't take another step, sonny boy!"

Tad halted. A plump old woman, a huge guitar strapped to her back, was down on her knees directly in his path.

She was muttering, slapping at the planks with her mottled hands. "I'll have it in a minute."

"Are you about to have some kind of attack?"

"Not on your life, sonny boy," she replied. "I'm searching for my left eye."

"How'd you—"

"That dumbell Washboard Willie gave me a heavy slap on the back by way of greeting," she said. "His nitwit arm played several bars of a waltz and my glaz eye went flying."

"Can I help you hunt?"

"Nope, thanks. I'm an old-fashioned soul. Certain parts of a woman's body are personal, I believe. That includes the. . . . Ho! there's the little dickens!" She scooped up something from the deck, inserted it in her face.

Tad extended a hand to help her rise. "I'm Tad . . . Jaxon, a guest of—"

"Know all about you." A smile spread across her broad face. "You no doubt recognize me as Mother Zarzarkas."

"Matter of fact, I don't. See, I'm offplanet so—"

"My ditties are famed all over this nitwit universe, sonny boy," the old woman told him. "Mother Zarzarkas, the Senile Bard of Esmeralda, the Sweet Folk Singer, the Guitar-Picking Granny."

"I'm not very musical, I guess." He shook his head.

"You don't have to be musical to appreciate me," she told him. "I make social comments. When I recorded 'Forced Retirement At Eighty Is Stupid Blues' my old guitar wasn't even in tune, but that tune sold ten million." She paused to poke his chest with a finger. "Do you mean to tell me you've never heard my biggest hit, the one about substandard housing? You've never heard 'Building Code Violations Rag'?"

"Don't think so, but as I said—"

"Civilization's worse blights are going to run right over you, sonny boy," she prophesied. "Unless you heed the warnings. Come on down to my cabin later and I'll sell you a batch of my hits."

"Yes, thanks, I will." He edged around her, entered the stage area of the swift-moving riverboat.

The juggler was gone, a small man in a dark one-piece suit held the stage. He had prickly dark hair, deep-set eyes, a hawkish nose. He was frowning at the backstage section at the moment, his gloved hands stroking each other anxiously. "You look fine, Altadena. Come on out."

"Keep your yurp in gear, Bobby," called an unseen girl from behind the backdrop.

Tad took a seat several rows from the footlights.

"She's always like this," the man on the stage said to him. "I know how to pick them. Tall, lovely in a cool and distant way and eternally late."

"I'm Tad Jaxon. We came aboard last night after—"

"Yes, I heard all about you and your adventures at the Belles Lettres. A perfect illustration of the godawful messes a woman can get you into."

"It wasn't exactly her—"

"My name is Bob Phantom. I'm the magician with this show, and you've probably never heard of me."

"No, I haven't."

The magician came forward, sat on the stage edge. "I'll tell you why. It's because of my fondness for a particular type of women. Tall, lovely in a cool distant way and unfaithful."

"I thought you said eternally late."

"Late usually because they're off being unfaithful. Altadena, we have to rehearse."

"Don't get your nork in an uproar, Bobby!"

"There's another factor," said Bob Phantom. "Consumers aren't awed by a magician who's called Bobby by his intimates. There's no mystery, no awe. Bobby."

"Don't a lot of people in show business change their names?"

"I'll never do that, it'd be a violation of my whole identity. Bob Phantom I was born, Bob Phantom I remain." He rested his gloved hands on his knees. "The thing which really annoys me is . . . I'm a real magician. You know, I have real powers."

"You do?"

"Altadena, are you ready?"

"Hold your grouts, Bobby!"

Bob Phantom lifted one hand, nodding at Tad. "I'll demonstrate one of my powers." His eyes shut for a few seconds, his fingertip traced a lazy circle in the air.

All at once a tall and lovely girl was on the stage, her left shoe dangling in her hand and a hair ribbon

hanging around her neck. "Showing off again?" she asked as she hopped to tug on her shoe. "I truly get tired of being teleported, Bobby. It really turns around my insides, as you well know."

"Tall and lovely," said Bob Phantom, "but uncaring."

"Think that was a trick?"

Tad jerked up straight. "Oh, I didn't hear you coming."

Jana Taine sat down next to him. "I can be quite sneaky at times. How are you feeling?"

"Relatively well."

"I came looking for you," the blonde girl said. "Thought you might want to have breakfast with me down in the galley."

Tad grinned at her. "Yes, I would," he answered.

Chapter 13

Trees circled the stone docking area at Siltville. A hundred or more low, thick-trunk trees, with globes of colored light strung in their twisting intertwined branches. As the showboat drifted in toward the twilight shore metal fingers tapped Tad's shoulder.

He turned away from the rail, expecting to encounter Electro. "Oh, hello, Washboard."

The one man band said, "Come backstage with me for a *twitty twit* minute, can you?"

"Sure, what's the problem?"

"It's the *twitty twit* commodore." Washboard gave himself a smack across the back of the neck. "My flute attachment is fritzed up." He administered two more smacks. "There that should *twit* take . . . well, it's a little better." He led Tad along the deck and around behind the stage.

Commodore Snow, a large chubby catman in a two-piece blue captain suit, was roaming fretfully across a strip of deck. In his right paw he clutched a raw turnip, which he was gnawing at. "I shouldn't let you hoodoo me, Will," he said. "The material is surefire."

"Not funny," said Washboard Will.

"It got big laughs in Fetid Landing, Seepage and Raw Sewage," the commodore said. "Those are all, as I shouldn't have to remind you, very savvy audience towns. If they laugh at you in Fetid Landing, Seepage and Raw Sewage, they'll fall off their seats in Siltville. That's an old theatrical adage, by the way."

Washboard shook his head, his whistles clacking together. "Didn't I win the Siltville Drama Critics Circle Award two years in a—"

"What can they know about drama? Giving a gaudy loving cup to a man wth a clarinet built into his—"

"They know what's funny. They know that much. They aren't going to laugh, or even snicker, over this opening monologue of yours, commodore."

Snow beckoned Tad to come closer. "You're a bright lad, I can see that, although this is the first time I've seen you conscious," he said. "You have a sense of humor, don't you?"

"Nearly everybody does."

"Exactly." With both paws he moved a folding chair over to Tad. "Sit down, relax, behave perfectly naturally. I'll run through my monologue, you give us your unbiased opinion."

Sitting, Tad glanced from the ship's captain to the one man band. "You want me to pretend I'm the audience?"

"The Siltville audience," amended Washboard. "The very discriminating Siltville audience, which will include at tonight's performance at least seven of th' nine members of the Siltville Dram—"

"Enough for the warmup," said Snow. "Let me get to the monologue."

Washboard made a slight bow. "Proceed," he said. "Tad, you laugh whenever it's funny."

"It's difficult, you know, to respond naturally when people are scrutinizing you."

"Make the best try you can." Commodore Snow cleared his throat, rubbed his paws together. "Do you think I need a nose, Will?"

"Skip the nose," advised the one man band. "The nose isn't going to help in Siltville."

"I wear, let me explain, young man, a very whimsical red bulb nose when I deliver the opening monologue."

"Does that notion strike you as funny?" Washboard inquired of Tad.

"I'd have to see it before I pass judgment."

"It won't take a minute for me to fetch it from my cabin."

"We're tying up at the Siltville dock," Washboard pointed out. "Do the monologue, so we can get to work revising it."

The commodore's cheek whiskers stood up; he made a growling sound. Finally he said, "This is a monologue about stookers, young man."

"Beg pardon?"

"Stookers . . . wangstix, diddlers."

"I don't think any of those words—"

"See commodore, he doesn't get it already and you've barely commenced."

"I mean pritzes, jabbers, diddywingers," continued Snow, his paws drawing vague pictures in the air. "What the blue blazes do they call a penis where you come from?"

"Oh, I see what you're getting at," said Tad. "Well, on Barnum the most used slang word would be—"

"Barnum?" Snow glared at Washboard Will. "This mooncalf is offplanet. What kind of ringer are you trying to foist on me? How's he going to be able to test my stuff?"

"Real humor is universal," said Washboard. "Knows no boundries, no frontiers. If something is truly funny it'll get a laugh in the farthest reaches of the galaxy. Now go ahead, and give him a sample of the dreadful stuff you're going to try to get laughs with tonight."

Commodore Snow smoothed down the fur on the top of his head. "Critics, you start listening to critics and this is what happens." He shuffled his booted feet, coughed into his paw. "Well, folks, it seems there was a quilptrapper who gets drunk on a visit to the big city. He's wandering the streets late at night when he realizes he has to take a weep. He sits down on the curb, unseams his baffler and wimps out his dangler." He paused, scrutinized Tad's face. "Are you following it so far?"

"I think I get it. Am I right in assuming, though, that the joke isn't over yet?"

"No, it's not over, no." Snow rubbed at his furry head again. "I'm deftly building up to the smash punch line. At any rate, two groutrunners happen along and decide to get prankish. This quiltrapper has fallen asleep on the curb, with his wanger still out. They tie a length of blue ribbon around his bonger, as a joke. Now the next morning he awakens, the quil-trappers does, and he notices . . . maybe you're right, Will. I should have had a giggle or two by this point. The little ribbon-tying business with my paws usually gets an appreciative chuckle."

"I'm telling you, commodore, we have to shift to new material."

"Let me try one more of my sure-fire wagstaff gags

on this young man." Snow gazed up at the darkening sky. "It seems this lizard man has a date with. . . . You do know, don't you, lizard men are reputed to possess exceptional quiffers?"

"I hadn't heard that, no. Is your joke based on that premise?"

"Yes. Yes, it is. This liz buys a new lecart and decides to take his sweetie for a . . . lecarts are small. That's an important point to keep in mind. Small vehicle, large lizard man noted for his extraodinary boofer. You might say that the premise of this little—"

"Two premises might be too many," suggested Tad.

"He and his sweetie go for a jaunt in the country. And the sweetie is getting pretty excited. When the liz finally stops the lecart she jumps right out and spreads a thermket on the swark and . . . you're frowning. Is there something else you don't understand?"

Tad said, "I was only wondering if this is going to be the old joke where the girl says, 'Hurry up before I get over this mood,' and he says—"

"It's not an old joke! It's a fresh new joke, written by me." The commodore put his furry fists on his hips. "Have you maybe seen my act previously?"

"Probably a different joke. The one I'm talking about we used to tell in Middle School back on Barnum. Except we didn't use lizards, we—"

"This is a lizard joke!"

"Ours used Venusians and the punchline was, 'I can't get out of this car until I get over my mood.' "

"Will, go down to my cabin and get the wig and dress," the commodore suddenly ordered.

"I wouldn't advise it," said the one man band.

"When nothing else works it's time to dress up in lady clothes," said Snow, with a determined nod of his head. "I'll open with my drag monologue. Never mind fetching it, I'll go myself. I'll use the red nose, too." With an anxious snort, he went trotting away.

"He's really got a fairly sound sense of humor," said Washboard Will. "The pressures of this business, though. . . ." He shrugged, and music came out of his knees as he followed the commodore away.

"My boy." Electro stepped up beside Tad.

Standing, he asked, "What is it? And why that outfit?"

The robot had donned a purple cloak and a floppy wide brim hat. "Another disguise, obviously," replied Electro, whispering. "Assumed so we can unobtrusively slip away during the first show tonight."

"Slip away?"

"It isn't safe, especially after all the frumus we kicked up in Fetid Landing, to stay aboard this craft much beyond nightfall."

"There's no indication anyone is wise to us."

"I wouldn't be certain of that, my boy," said the robot, his voice even quieter. He tapped his purple-clad chest with a forefinger. "I've been able to determine someone on this barge has been using a radio communicator, my sensors show that beyond a doubt."

"Radio? For what?"

"I can't monitor it; Cosmo never got around to building in that particular ability," said Electro. "My guess would be someone has alerted Joshua to our whereabouts."

"Sounds unlikely to me, but if you want to go, okay," said Tad. "I'll tell Jana, so she can get ready."

Electro restrained him with a hand on his arm. "She may be the one who's informing on us," he said.

Chapter 14

"I'm tired of people calling me a mooncalf, whatever that is," said Tad. "I'm tired of people trying out their routines and their theories on me. You don't like Jana, okay. I do. You haven't any proof she—"

"But I have, my boy." Electro bonked the side of his glistening skull. "My detectors took me right to the spot where the radio sending set is stashed."

"You mean it's in Jana's cabin?"

"Not in her cabin, in Mother Zarzarkas' cabin. Jana, however, was in there."

"Paying a social visit to the old lady, probably."

"The old dear wasn't even there," said Electro. "She was down in the engine room entertaining the crew with a ballad entitled, I believe, 'Renegotiate Your Contract Every Two Years.' Catchy tune, although an oversimplified view of labor-management relati—"

"You still don't know Jana is trying to turn us in to Cousin Joshua," said Tad, angry. "You trailed her around, found her in somebody else's cabin. You're building a whole halfass theory on—"

"What was she doing in there, then?"

"Here's a better question. Why does that doddering old folk singer have a radio set?"

"Mother Z may be an accomplice."

"What would Jana gain by turning us in, by betraying us? Cousin Joshua's people will drag her straight back to her husband."

"If she has a husband," said Electro. "We have only her word for it. Everything the young lady claims may well be false, simply a cover story."

"Sure, she's really a spy planted by my cousin." Tad shook his head, throwing the robot a disgusted look. "He's so clever he got her to the Belles Lettres inn two whole days before we even thought about taking off from Foghill."

Electro said, "I am only suggesting she could by something other than what she pretends. The fight in the saloon, the goons attempting to carry her off could have been stage dressing, my boy. Bish, though a one-time man of the cloth, may have handed us a line of baloney. He recovered, you'll recall, impressively fast from the stunbeam used on him."

"Because the robot was old and out of shape."

"Possibly."

"Cousin Cosmo built a real paranoid streak into you." Tad started walking away from the backstage area.

"I was designed to look after things, to be a guardian if need be."

Tad strode rapidly along the deck. "I'm not all that certain I need a guardian."

"You need something," said Electro, close on his heels. "If you were on your own in this caper you'd be back at Foghill eating bread crusts by now. Your attempts to handle situations have resulted in blows to the skull and then a blast from a stungun."

Tad didn't reply. He pushed his way through the crewmen who were letting down a gangplank. Already several dozen customers were lining up on the stone dock.

The door to Jana's cabin was slightly open. When Tad knocked it swung inward. "Jana?"

"Caution, my boy. Use caution."

Tad went into the small room. The girl wasn't there. "Do you have any idea where she is?"

"Let us try Mother Z's cabin."

"Okay, we'll look there."

"Four doors down this very corridor."

Tad got no answer when he knocked on the old folk singer's door. He took hold of the knob, then shoved on the door. It opened.

"Goodness, these old ears are failing me. I didn't hear your knock." The old woman was standing wide-legged in the center of the cabin, holding her guitar by its neck.

Sprawled on the floor was Jana.

"What the hell did you do to her?"

"Who? Oh, you mean Mrs. Taine." Mother Zarzarkas made a fluttering motion with her free hand. "I was about to holler for the commodore. The young lady suddenly fainted. Very odd."

Tad knelt beside the unconscious blonde. "There's blood on her scalp. You must have—"

"Whoa!" Electro's right arm swung out, caught the guitar before the old woman could bop Tad over the head with it. "You should have more respect for your instrument."

"Take a hairy leap for yourself," said Mother Zarzarkas, tugging to get possession of the guitar. She let go of it suddenly, jerked a blaster pistol out of her dress bosom.

Tad jumped, tackling her while slapping at the weapon with the side of his hand.

The guitar, flung aside by Electro, cracked into three pieces, strings twanging when it hit the cabin wall.

The robot pointed his left little finger at the gray-haired folk composer. A misty line of blue light jumped from the fingertip to Mother Zarzarkas' head.

"Yowie!" she exclaimed in a deep voice before dropping to the floor in a deep sleep.

Tad returned to the girl. "Jana, try to—"

"I'm okay . . . or nearly so." Her eyes opened. "I shouldn't have let him smack me from behind."

Tad said, "Yeah, Mother Zarzarkas is a guy, isn't he?"

"One of Rhymer Industries' crack espionage agents," said Jana, sitting up with Tad's help.

"You mean he works for RI? And he tried to conk me with that damn guitar."

"He's on Joshua's side, not yours," reminded Electro as he crossed to a closet and opened it. "Yes, herein lies the radio set." He demolished it with one kick of his metal foot.

"He's notified them about you two," said Jana. "I heard him, while hiding in the washroom over there. Unfortunately he discovered me and bopped me a good one before I could get away clear."

"How come Cousin Joshua has an agent on this showboat?" asked Tad. "He couldn't have known we were going to travel this way."

"This agent's chief job is to spy on various river town activites, especially the doings of RI's rivals," said Jana, standing. "He recognized you, contacted RI. They confirmed you were missing and wanted."

"How'd you know he was a fake?"

"When I was still in the good graces of my husband and the Rhymer forces," answered Jana, "I met this guy, when he wasn't in costume. After we'd been onboard awhile I recognized him. I figured he might be someone sent out to grab me, so I tried a bit of espionage work on my own. With not too terrific results, as you may have noticed."

"We took care of him," said Tad, "and we know what he—"

"What is their alleged plan?" Electro asked the girl. "What is Joshua Rhymer planning to do about us?"

Jana said, "There'll be a gang of men coming aboard when we dock at Siltville. They'll be posing as customers come to see the show." She glanced toward the open cabin door. "Have we docked already?"

"Yep, while you were knocked out."

"Then they're on the boat by now," said Jana. "We're as good as caught."

"Far from it," said Electro.

Chapter 15

"A splendid bit of work, I must admit." Electro, one hand clasping the opposite elbow, took a backward step. "You both look amazingly lizardlike."

"I feel that way, too." Jana turned to inspect her disguise in the wall mirror. "You're a whiz at getting that scaly effect, Electro."

"Yes, you're absolutely right."

Tad scratched at the back of his green scaly hand. "You really think we can fool a whole gang of thugs?" Both he and the girl had been converted into fairly convincing facsimiles of lizard people.

Jana was, using a needle and thread found among Mother Zarzarkas' effects, taking up the hem on the purple cloak the robot had loaned her. "I bet we'll be able to fool the whole lot of them," she said. "What sort of disguise are you going to use, Electro?"

The robot bent, tugged the wig off the slumbering RI agent. "I'll become a sweet-tempered old lady." He plopped the wig on his skull, stepped closer to the mirror to change his gleaming face to a semblance of wrinkled flesh.

"This Rhymer Industries agent recognized us." Tad adjusted the floppy purple hat the robot had insisted he wear. "Most likely others will, too."

"He recognized us because we made the error of appearing undisguised,'" said Electro, rapidly changing his appearance. "My fault, letting down our guard. We should have remained in makeup."

"You couldn't have," said Tad, "anticipated an RI spy on board this showboat."

"A person of my abilities should have, my boy." He cocked his head far to the left, far to the right. "A striking replica of the Sweet Singer of Senile Songs." He stepped over to the fallen agent, undressed him quickly and slipped into his garments. "Ah, three more pistols concealed on him. A very crafty chap." Electro began prowling the cabin, peeking into closets, squinting under the bunk. "Ah, exactly what I seek. The old dear carried a spare." He hauled a second guitar from beneath the rumpled bed.

"You aren't going to need that," said Tad.

"It adds to the illusion." The robot slung the instrument over his broad back. "I will be Mother Zarzarkas, going ashore in the company of two of my ardent local fans. My objective is to pay a brief visit to their clubhouse. Sounds plausible, looks plausible."

"You make an enormous old lady."

"I'll affect a convincing and charming stoop."

"He looks fine." Jana placed the modified cloak over her slim shoulders. "We all do. Relax, Tad, and let's assume we're going to con whoever your cousin sends to capture us."

"A little while ago you were gloomy, talking about how we were all of us trapped."

The girl laughed. "My outlook does tend to

fluctuate, doesn't it? Annoyed the hell out of my husband." She shrugged. "Right at the moment I'm optimistic. Okay?"

"We'll venture now into the corridor." Electro gathered his skirt up, tiptoed to the cabin door and opened it. There was no activity in the passway. "We'll begin our act. Goodness, I never imagined I had so many admirers in a dinky place such as Siltville." He stepped out of the cabins.

"We have a hundred plus members, mother," said Jana, following. "Each and every one crazy over your recordings."

"Oh, it gladdens my old heart to realize my music is reaching so many fine young people."

The three of them moved out of the corridor and onto the deck. The audience section was already over half full, with a line of patrons coming single file up the gangplank. The sky was completely dark now, blurred slightly with mist.

"Red lizard men over there," said Tad close to the robot's ear, nodding at the seated audience.

"An entire row of them," amended the robot. "We can't be sure all red lizards in this forlorn part of the planet are in the pay of your cousin. Nonetheless, the sooner we disembark from the craft the better."

"Ha, just who I want!" Commodore Snow, dressed now in a style similar to Elector's and sporting a red bulb nose, came hurrying up to the disguised robot.

"Goodness me, commodore, you seem all in a dither."

"Washboard Will's having stomach trouble," explained the agitated captain. "Which, as you know, means he can't use his entire rhythm section. You'll have to do the opening spot tonight, Mother Zarzarkas."

"Dear me," said Electro in his exact imitation of

the folk singer's voice. "I've promised these two adoring lizard youths to pop over to town for a—"

"You can do that later." Snow got a grip on Electro's arm, started urging him along the deck.

Electro dragged his feet, halting their progress. "Commodore, I didn't become the most beloved balladeer in the universe by stiffing my fans or—"

"What's bothering the old broad?"

"Don't she want to entertain us?"

"Maybe a few smacks across the choppers will change her mind."

Two red lizard men and an albino catman had come tromping up the gangplank. They circled Commodore Snow and Electro, scowling.

"Them," Tad whispered to the girl. "They were at the inn."

"We can wait until you sing," said Jana, loudly. "You have to please all your fanatical admirers, after all."

"Yeah, that's right," agreed a lizard man.

"This liz pussy hit the scroog right square on the bonko," observed the albino catman. "So let's hear the old quiff do her stuff. Right now!"

"This is certainly gratifying." Electro put one arm around Jana and the other around Tad. "You two little fanatics can wait backstage for me. Soon as I strut my stuff, we'll pop over to your lovely clubhouse. If you gentlemen will step aside, please."

"Sure thing, granny."

When they were clear of the goons Electro said, "We should have run for it. I could have stunned the lot of them while—"

"We don't know how many others there are," said Jana. "Or how many weapons they have. A sudden exit will probably bring down a whole troop on us.

We're better off letting them think you're Mother Zarzarkas."

"They know Mother Zarzarkas is a Rhymer Industries spy," said Tad. "So they must believe you're on their side."

Electro made a throat clearing sound. "Perhaps their violent insistence on my performing is some kind of good-natured lout kidding. Let us hope so."

As they entered the backstage area Tad asked, "You can play the guitar, can't you?"

"I'm proficient on all instruments," Electro assured him. "You ought to hear me on the pipe organ."

"We want the show!"

"Let's have the flapping entertainment!"

"Where's the old broad?"

Commodore Snow appeared. "Sophisticated audience, is it? A gaggle of low-life rowdies is what sits out there," he said, growling some. "I'm tempted to go back to my boofer monologue." He stroked his furry chin meditatively. "Though I might do it in drag, thereby getting the best of both routines." He gave Electro an encouraging pat on the arm, then winced. "You've got an impressively solid upper arm, Mother."

"Guitar strumming builds me up."

"Okay, get out there and do a few of your hits. See if you can get them in a receptive mood for a monologue about dorks." He loped away, picked up a backstage microphone to announce the impending advent of Mother Zarzarkas.

"There's only one thing which gives me concern over this impersonation," said Electro, unslinging his guitar.

Tad asked, "What?"

"I don't know even one of Mother Z's ditties."

Chapter 16

Shielded by a curtain, Jana scanned the audience. "Twenty-five . . . twenty-six," she said.

"You're not certain, though," said Tad.

"I'm pretty sure I can spot a thug when I see one," she replied. "The whole front row and the second row up until the crow woman in the maroon shift are composed of hoodlums, along with nearly half the third row. I'm also fairly certain those three in the fourth row over there are, too."

"The middle one is the drama critic for the *Siltville Bulletin*," said Bob Phantom, who was standing nearby. "I don't believe we've met. I'm Bob Phantom, the obscure magician."

Tad said, "I'm Tad . . . in disguise."

Bob Phantom narrowed his left eye. "Why, so you are. You and the young lady going to be part of the show?"

"We hope not," said Jana.

"What it is," Tad told the magician, "we're sort of

in trouble, Mr. Phantom. Quite a few people want to do us harm. So it's important we get off this boat."

"Loitering backstage isn't helping any, is it?"

"We have to wait for my robot."

"Where is he?"

"Out there on stage, trying to impersonate Mother Zarzarkas."

"I envy you," said Bob Phantom with a sigh. "Being associated with someone who has such a yearning to perform, who goes on with the show even when there's danger. Altadena would never do that. I can hardly drag her onstage most evenings. Even when I use my teleportation gift she—"

"Boo!"

"Lousy!"

"Stinko! Phew!"

"Electro's not going over very well," said Jana.

"Rotten!"

"Fooey!"

"Unconvincing and shallow!"

Electro was nearly through his third ballad. He ceased in midsong. "I can see you clunks don't appreciate sea chanties."

"Boo!"

"Give us songs of social import!"

"You buffoons don't know social import from your elbow," said the robot. "Now hush up while I conclude 'The Lighthouse Keeper's Only Daughter.' Ahum. Rum tiddy tum, rum tiddy tee, I love Lulu Belle and she loves me. Sing along if you like."

"We don't like!"

"Mediocre!"

"Inept finger-picking!"

"Toss a cobblestone at him, mate!"

"Good idear!"

Bonk!

"Damn," said Tad, "that brick hit him smack on the head."

"Making a telltale metallic thud," said Jana.

"Rum tiddy tiddle, rum tiddy tawdle, I can tell my Lulu by the way she waddles."

"Terrible rhyme!"

"An odd sound her old skonce made, mate!"

"Aye, so it was. Give her another one, bucko!"

Kathunk!

"That ain't no old skwack! That's a blinking robot in disguise!"

"Somebody swipe my drag gimmick?" inquired Commodore Snow as he came hurrying through the wings. "That goes against the code of the theater."

"Back, you dimbulbs!" warned Electro. He tossed aside his guitar, rolled up a sleeve. He aimed a hand, fingers wide, at the restive audience. "I'll stun the first manjack who tries to assault me."

"Let's get this blooming gadget, mates!"

"Let him have it!"

A wave of a dozen burly men came scrambling over the footlights.

Zizzle!

Zzitz!

Zzang!

Though several fell stunned, more leaped onto the stage.

"Seems the whole damn audience is in your cousin's pay." Jana took hold of Tad's hand.

That distracted him for a few seconds. "There's too many of them, they'll overwhelm Electro."

"Maybe we can get away while—"

"No, I can't abandon him." He turned to Bob Phantom. "Can you really do that teleportation stunt or is it a trick?"

"I can really teleport objects and people. It's a gift,"

answered the magician. "I inherited my telekinetic powers from my maternal grandm—"

"Can you use it now?"

"This seems an unlikely time to want to see me teleport Altadena from the dressing room to—"

"I want you to use it on us. Can you teleport our robot and me and Jana off this damn showboat?"

New dark rings formed under Bob Phantom's eyes as he considered. "Yes, I believe so. I've never done three at once before, nor anyone as bulky as your robot companion. Still, it's a challenge and I see no reason why I can't succeed. You want to go right now, I suppose?"

Out on the stage nine men were piled atop the toppled Electro.

"Yes, that would be helpful."

"You may feel a little initial unease in your stomachs," said Bob Phantom. "At least Altadena always complains of that, but then she's a born complainer. Tall, lovely in a cool and distant sort of way and always bitching." His eyes closed, one hand made lazy circles.

"Can he really . . ." began Jana.

Dark trees rose up all around them. High, straight trees stretching up into the black night sky.

"Hey, this is terrific." Laughing, Jana hugged him. "We got away."

Tad reluctantly eased away from her. "But," he said, "where's Electro?"

Chapter 17

Thump!

Thunk!

"That sounds familiar." Tad spun toward the distant noise. "It's him."

"How many times have you heard Electro fall over in a wilderness?" inquired Jana.

"I know the sound a robot makes landing hard." He was heading into the dark rows of trees, aimed at the spot the metallic thumps had come from.

"But this could be something else." The slim girl caught up with him, taking hold of his hand. "We better proceed carefully."

"Suppose you're right."

After a moment Jana said, "Any idea what part of the country we're in?"

"The outskirts of Siltville, probably."

She said, "I visited Siltville several times with my husband. This doesn't look like the outskirts."

"I should have asked Bob Phantom where he was

planning to send us," said Tad. "At the time, though, I was more concerned—"

"Stop a minute," cautioned Jana.

"What?"

"Listen."

The drumming of hoofbeats was growing nearby.

"We must be close to a roadway," whispered Jana.

Eyes narrowed, Tad glanced all around. He saw nothing but the high dark trees.

The sounds of riders increased.

"Death to smut!"

"Repress bawdy stuff!"

"Burn all filth vendors!"

Angry sounds came rolling across the night forest from somewhere on their left. Soon the cries died, the hoofbeats faded.

"Odd hour for a parade," remarked the girl.

"Well, we're not smut vendors so it hasn't anything to do with us. Let's find Electro."

As they resumed hiking Jana said, "Wonder who those fellows were."

"Long as they're not from RI, I don't care."

"I only hope we didn't land in the middle of a skirmish or a—"

"Slow and then halt, folks." A lightrod had all at once blossomed directly in their path. The beam sought and locked in on Tad and the girl. "We usually don't find lizes with them, especially two so young."

"Actually we're not lizards at all." Tad brought up his scaly green hand to wipe away some of the makeup from his face. "It's only—"

"No swift moves, lad," warned the unseen man beyond the glaring light. "Let the hand return to your side. Very good."

Jana asked, "Who are you?"

"You ought to know that, lass. Seeing as how you've come here to hunt us down and set us afire."

"We have no intention of setting anyone on fire," said Tad. "We're hunting for my robot who—"

"Ha, so now you're using mechanized attackers on us, eh? Not bad enough you come galloping through fields and forest on great ugly grouts and powerful horse. No, now you must send mechanisms—"

"Listen, we're more or less lost in this woodland," Tad tried to explain. "Whoever you may be, we don't contemplate doing you any harm. As soon as we locate Electro and get our bearings we—"

"Are you claiming," asked the unseen man, "you never head of *Swill?*"

Tad shook his head. "Some sort of animal food?"

"Come, come, lad, you're feigning too much stupidity. Since near everyone knows about *Swill, the Magazine of Disgusting Sex.*"

"Oh, that *Swill.* Sure, I saw copies in our dorm back on Barnum but—"

"Your hidden printing plant," said Jana. "It's around here somewhere, isn't it?"

"As you already well know, lass."

Tad turned to the girl. "*Swill* has some sort of hidden presses?"

"Since the whole *Swill* chain of magazines is outlawed on most of the planets in the Barnum System," she answered, "they have to use a secret setup. Apparently we've wandered into its vicinity."

"They've mistaken us for some of those guys who went by yelling slogans."

"Not convincing," said the man with the lightrod. "Ugo, herd them onto the path."

Tad hopped forward when an unexpected blaster barrel prodded him in the back. "We really have to find our robot, and we don't have—"

"Move it," urged Ugo in a husky voice.

"The publisher wants to talk to you two vigilantes." Their captor, who was a thin catman of forty, returned to the tile-walled room he had deposited them in an hour earlier.

Tad indicated his face with both hands. "Look, we're not lizards any longer. It was only a disguise to—"

"Makes no diff what your species, lad. We get rid of spies and vigilantes of all kinds and categories," replied the catman. "Otherwise we couldn't maintain the spirit of press freedom which is so essential to us."

"My name is Tad Rhymer. You must have heard of Rhymer—"

"We have that, yes." The catman's yellow eyes slitted down. "Joshua Rhymer's put a good deal of capital and effort into wiping us out. He claims *Swill* and our sister magazine, *Bilge, the Magazine of Depraved Lust,* must be squelched. We didn't realize he was sending members of the clan directly against us."

"His Cousin Joshua loathes him," put in Jana. "That's why we're running, to get away from the old codger."

The catman moved to the magazine rack which was the single piece of furniture in the white room. "You didn't even look at any of our mags," he said, disappointed. "We've got advance copies of *Lewd* here and *Swill Forum, the Magazine of Disgusting Confessions.* You have to admit, even if you are fanatically opposed to free expression of sexual standards differing from your own, that this is a socko cover on *Swill Forum.* Am I right?"

"Socko," said Jana. "Though it could have been a shade more disgusting."

"You think so?" The catman plucked the magazine

off the rack, held it at arm's length, whiskers flickering. "No, I think this is one of the most completely disgusting covers we've ever done. If it were any more disgusting we'd cross the boundaries of good taste." He rolled the magazine up, tapped against his thigh with it. "You see, despite our underground operations, we put a good deal of effort into market research. With this particular *Swill Forum* cover we did considerable testing. We smuggled advance proofs into the Home For The Sexually Goofy on Murdstone, the Retired Rapists Retreat on Malagra—and there, by the way, a single swift glance at the cover inspired three of the old boys to resume their careers. We even, and this is quite a coup, tracked down the notorious Bert the Slasher, better known as the Unspeakable Crimes Man, to his lair on Esmeralda and Bert gave us a rave reaction. You notice we feature a direct quote from him smack across the cover. 'Aargh . . . lemme hold it . . . aiee . . . it does strange things to me . . . grrr . . . blood . . . lace pants . . . kill kill kill! (Signed) Berton "The Slasher" Plaut, AKA The Unspeakable Crimes Man.' A true smasher of a cover." He arranged the magazine back in its place in the rack. "Enough publishing gossip, let's keep our appointment with the publisher."

Outside the white room was a white corridor. This corridor led to another white corridor.

"Do you know who the publisher is?" Tad asked the girl.

"Nope, never heard of him."

The catman said, "The publisher of all our magazines and books is Dr. Donald 'Dirty Mind' Denslow. I'd better caution you now that if you laugh at him when you first encounter him he's likely to kill you on the spot."

Chapter 18

They didn't laugh, neither Tad nor Jana.

"Ironic," said Dirty Mind Denslow. "No doubt that's what you're thinking. Go ahead, snicker, chortle and laugh."

"We'd rather not," said Tad, nodding at the blaster pistol in one of the publisher's hands.

"It is ironic," went on Denslow. "Something my many critics delight in twitting me about. Would you like to wash your hands?"

"No, thanks," said Tad.

"Take your picture? Three poses for a buck."

"Why," inquired Jana, "have you assumed this . . . persona?"

"Fate," replied the publisher. "Like a towel?" Another of his white metal arms rose, a fresh white towel waving from it. "Up until three years ago I was a perfectly normal, strikingly handsome purveyor of degrading filth. If you don't need a towel, how about thrusting your hands under my hot air nozzle for a few seconds? It's free."

"We'll pass," Tad said.

"Three years ago I made the fatal mistake of attending a Swillcon," said Denslow out of the voicebox in his white metal chest. "All around the known universe, on every habitable planet, there are fans of my publications. Do you have any notion, by the way, what a challenge that is? To have to arouse the lowest, most rotten sexual urges in everybody from the owlmen of Murdstone to the snakemen of Jupiter. Have you ever considered how difficult it is to come up with a pinup centerfold which will disgust a lizard man, a catman and a humanoid? Yes, and you still have to be artistic about it. Few besides your humble servant, Dirty Mind Denslow, have consistently achieved any measure of success."

"How come you ended up as a washroom attendant robot?" asked Jana.

Behind them the catman gasped. "Thin ice," he murmured.

"A very bright young woman," said Denslow, chuckling inside his mechanical self. "Perhaps we can use you as a Degraded Sex Object of the Month before we exterminate you. Or possibly after. We'll see." He steepled the fingers of a few of his white hands. "As I was saying, I had been cajoled into appearing as a GOH at a Swillcon. That's Guest of Honor, in case you weren't aware. It was the big 10th Annual Swillcon on the planet Malagra, sometimes known as the pesthole of the universe. We have our biggest concentration of fans there. So I broke my cardinal rule and surfaced long enough to attend. Quite naturally all Swillcons are held on the sly. In spite of very efficient security measures a large faction of smut hunters got wind I was going to make the keynote speech at the Swillcon luncheon. When I rose to speak, following the traditional Unspeakably Vile Lingerie Fashion Show, I was rudely set upon by well over two dozen brutal anti-intellectuals armed with clubs."

The catman guard was softly sobbing now, sniffling into his paw. "A sad day for publishing," he said.

"Before my devoted admirers could pull off my attackers, dismember them and dice them into chunks, I was already cruelly damaged," continued Denslow. "Most of my body was in ruined shape, all that was still functioning at all was my magnificent brain, the same brain which had conceived the entire *Swill* empire. Remind me to gift you with a pair of disgusting cufflinks, young man. For the young lady a Repuslive Sex Object locket and matching earrings. To continue. Fortunately for the cause of a free press, one of my most devoted fans at that luncheon happened to be the noted transplant whiz, Dr. John 'Thumbs' Fairfield. He leaped to my aid, as soon as he had pulled up his trousers and detached all the chains, leather thongs and barbed wire from about his person. A brilliant man, Thumbs assured me that, if we worked fast and were very lucky, he could transfer my brain into another body."

"A miracle it was," muttered the catman.

Denslow said, "Strangely enough there was a lack of volunteers. I must admit I was disappointed, since I'd made considerable effort and taken great risks to be their GOH. We almost got a young fellow who specialized in tattooing obscene pictures on his flesh to donate his body, such as it was, but his mother, a striking woman with a knee fetish, wouldn't sign the necessary papers. Time was running out, my life was ebbing, my great brain drew ever closer to being stilled forever."

"Tragic," said the catman.

"Then Thumbs came up with the inspired suggestion that if we couldn't rope in a human host, a robot would do. This didn't initially appeal to me, being as I was a man much given to lewd fleshly pleasures and degrading and demeaning physical acts. However, I decided I owed it to myself and my myriad admirers to keep the most enlightened publishing mind in the universe going. Thus I agreed with my last conscious words to having my brain placed in the body of a robot."

"Couldn't you," asked Jana, "have picked a better looking robot?"

"My thought exactly when I awoke to find Thumbs Fairfield had entrusted my brain to the skull of the robot washroom attendant from the convention hotel," said Denslow. "Remind me to squirt you with perfume later. I contain three different scents. Apparently the hotel management, reluctant about the Swillcon to begin with and not put in a better mood by my near murder at the hands of crazed purity vigilantes, was quite uncooperative when Thumbs attempted to purchase one of their robot staff. If my fans hadn't threatened to commit acts of incredible sexual malice on the entire human staff, the hotel wouldn't even have parted with the washroom robot. It became a case of, as I've often told people since, any port in a storm." He gestured with three of his hands. "Which is why you see me before you in this unfortunate state."

"You have to admit it's disgusting," said Jana. "That ought to appeal to someone of your tastes, Mr. Denslow."

"Yes, that is a modest benefit," admitted the *Swill* publisher. "A few of the women I've had encounters with claim my new format is so repulsive they arrive at new and thrilling levels of sexual distaste when they're with me. Now that I've concluded my little autobiographical interlude, we'll proceed with the quest—"

Blam!

The room's white door came dancing off its hinges. It clanged into the wall, fell over and smacked the floor with a resounding whoosh.

"Good evening, all," said Electro from the threshold. "I know I'm late, but I had to stun an endless stream of nitwits to get here."

"What's the big idea of . . . say, don't I know you?" asked Denslow.

"You have the advantage of me, sir. I don't recall ever having met a washroom—"

"You didn't have that gray curly hair then, but—"

"Oops, I neglected to remove the last traces of an earlier disguise." Electro whipped the Mother Zarzarkas wig off his skull.

"Electro!" cried Denslow.

The robot took a few steps toward the publisher. "From the way you shout my name I get the notion we were once—"

"I'm Denslow, Dirty Mind Denslow," said Denslow forlornly. "Doomed to walk the earth in a robot body."

"Oh, there are worse fates."

Tad said, "How come you know him, Electro? Or do you?"

"Yes, Denslow is a friend of your Cousin Cosmo. He paid frequent furtive visits to Foghill in the days when—"

"This partially disguised mooncalf is kin of Cosmo Rhymer?"

"Exactly," replied Electro.

"Well, then," said Denslow, "I can't very well shoot any of you."

"For old time's sake, you ought not to," advised Electro.

Chapter 19

Dawn light came racing through the jungle, scattering mist and turning everything swiftly green. "The chap had never lifted a mechanism of my size and weight before," Electro was explaining. "Prior to Bob Phantom's teleporting of me the heaviest object he'd ever moved was a hefty aunt of his who—"

"I don't think we should have accepted *Swill's* hospitality," said Tad as he followed the huge robot along the overgrown pathway. "Spending the night there was—"

"I never require rest myself," said Electro. "You tots, however, were in need of a night's repose."

"We lost a lot of time," Tad complained.

"Don't let it unsettle you," advised Jana, who was walking close beside him.

The robot said, "Once we reach this abandoned Underground Rapid Transit System I'm leading us to we'll solve our transportation problems. Its very name implies speed and—"

"I didn't like the furniture in the *Swill* setup," said Tad. "That's another reason I wasn't too cheered by having to sleep there."

"Granted," said Electro, "few people have spent a night in a bed shaped like an intimate part of the female anatomy but—"

"Female?" said Jana. "Oh, then you fellows must have had different furniture in your room."

"What was . . . no, never mind. I don't want to hear about it." Tad scowled.

"Speaking of *Swill*," said the blonde girl, "you were going to explain how you came to arrive and rescue us when you did, Electro."

"Since Tad heard most of my explanation last evening I hesitate—"

"Go ahead and tell her."

"I'd very much like to hear the story," added Jana.

"Your character has developed and broadened considerably since we first encountered you, young lady," said the robot approvingly. "Now where was I? Ah, yes, on the deck of the showboat facing an audience singularly uninterested in marine ballads. Bob Phantom experienced no trouble in teleporting you two away from there and into the jungle. With me, however, he encountered some technical difficulties. Eventually, with a bit of advice from me, he was able to accomplish the necessary teleportation. Moderately distracted by the extra effort required as well as the attacking louts, Bob Phantom dropped me approximately a mile and a quarter South of where he sent you. As fate would have it I landed smack in the midst of a herd of shugs. Perhaps you aren't aware that shugherders lead a rather isolated life, especially when it comes to companionship of the opposite sex. The expression 'Horny as a shugherder' grows out of this well-known situation. At any rate, I came thumping down in the middle of four hundred woolly shugs and six lonesome shugherders. Dressed as a lady, as I was at that moment, I produced quite an . . . . Trouble!" His head clicked back, eyes scanning the pale dawn sky above them.

Tad stared upward. "A skyvan."

"That's a Rhymer Industries ship," added Jana. "I know that color scheme."

The robot nodded. "They're searching for us," he announced. "My, that's interesting. Seems they already have copies of your body emanation charts." His head nodded three more times. "Efficient rascal, your Cousin J."

"They'll probably catch us, then," said Tad. "RI has developed all kinds of detecting gear. The skyvan should be loaded with it."

Slowly Electro rubbed his metal hands together. "Joshua's major mistake is underestimating my abilities," he said. "We'll be undetectable for a few hours anyway. Enough time, let us trust, to get underground and out of range."

"What about the detecting gear?" Tad jabbed a finger into the air.

"My boy, I have just rendered it all on the fritz. None of their equipment is now, inexplicably to their halfwit organic brains, operating." He tapped his massive chest, producing an echoing series of thumps. "One of the numerous gifts bestowed on me by my creator is the ability to kibosh mechanisms at a distance. Come along, children. Even humans can repair things if they work at it long enough."

"I'm not helping your cause much," said Jana as they hurried on after the striding robot. "My husband's people have probably teamed up with your cousin's crew. All I've done is add to the number of vexations."

"Cousin Joshua will keep after me whether I'm with you or not," he told the girl, taking hold of her arm. "If you're planning to suggest separating, don't."

She laughed softly. "Okay, all right. We'll remain a team," she said. "And if later on you . . . well, never mind."

"You haven't," he said, deciding to bring up something he'd long wanted to, "really told me much about . . . about your marriage."

"No, I haven't," said Jana.

"Up until now I haven't been the kind of guy who pried much into people's lives. You know, I felt I was a kid more or less and you didn't go asking grownups what they were up to. At school, with other guys I sat in on a lot of bull sessions where we . . . the point is, I feel concerned about you, Jana."

"Yes, I know you do." She placed her hand over his where it rested on her arm. "Thing is, Tad, I'm really not an admirable person at all. When I was a little girl my mother used to read me a story book . . . I don't remember the name of it. The little boy it was about continually got into fantastic messes, one after the other. When his mother came to rescue him, one of his friends would explain to her, 'He brought it on himself.' A good motto for me. She brought it on herself."

"Everybody gets into a bad situation once in awhile," said Tad. "But I don't believe anything can lock you into a lifelong path of bad times."

"You're young."

"Come on, you only have a few years' lead on me. Hardly enough of a span for you to try playing the ancient wise person with me."

"If you knew how I'd spent those few years you—"

"We better halt," suggested Electro, doing just that.

Tad realized he'd been concentrating on the girl

beside him and ignoring the jungle ahead. "What are they?" he asked.

"Person-eating tharks," answered Electro.

Two of the huge killer cats were on the trail some hundred yards in front of them. Pale green animals with fangs showing and tails switching.

"Can you," inquired Tad, "deal with them?"

"Yes, we've nothing to—"

"Bangalla! Bangalla!"

From the branches directly above came a resounding cry.

Chapter 20

"Bangalla! Bangalla!"

With another booming cry a large muscular man in an animal-skin loincloth came dropping out of the trees. He landed square on the back of one of the tharks.

The other beast gave out a startled snarl, its fur rose and it went galloping away into the early morning jungle.

The nearly naked man struggled with the remaining thark, attempting to get a neck-breaking hold on it. The thark seemed intent only on joining its retreating mate.

"Stay still," urged the jungle man.

"Bangalla! Bangalla!" There was another shout from above, a second jungle man came plummeting down out of the trees. He hit a few feet from the struggle.

"Don't need you, Mort," grunted the jungle man who was tangling with the unhappy thark.

His brother wiped grass stains off an elbow. "Thought there were two of the darn things, Dik."

"Well, there were," said Dik, panting. "Except that I . . . well, I scared one off."

"Bangalla! Bangalla!" A third jungle man dropped from the tree branches. A ringer for the other two, he hit directly onto the back of the jungle man and the thark.

This caused the wrestling jungle man to lose his hold, thus enabling the thark to dash away.

"Now see, Jerry," said Dik, squatted on the trail, "you come nosing in and you scare off the only really good challenge we've had in—"

"Me?" Jerry put hands on his bronzed hips. "You two seem to have forgotten it was my turn. Yes, my turn."

"No, if anything it was me who got screwed out of a turn," said Mort, brushing his long dark hair back from his handsome brow. "See, you got the rogue grout who was terrorizing the village, Jer. Then Dik took care of the—"

"The rogue grout was two months ago," cut in Jerry. "You're not trying to tell me I'm supposed to wait two lousy months before I—"

"Could be," said Dik, massaging his side, "there's not enough work for *three* jungle men in this part of the—"

"Oh, boy, here it comes again." Jerry gave a scornful chuckle. "You're going to suggest I quit so—"

"You could retire and live quite comfortably," Mort told him. "The money from the ivory we found in the elephant's graveyard provides plenty—"

"Oh, sure, live on that and desert the family business." Jerry shook his head. "Boy, if dad could see you guys now he'd—"

"Good morning, gentlemen," said Electro, leaving

the girl and Tad and moving closer to the bickering jungle men. "We appreciate your frightening off those tharks for us."

"Manners," said Jerry to his brothers. "There's another thing dad was always trying to instill in you dolts. Here you let our guests stand around while—"

"I was wrestling the damn thark," reminded Dik. "I was busy doing what a jungle man is supposed to do, whereas you two bumpkins were falling out of trees and—"

"If that poor thark hadn't broken your fall you'd have—"

"Forgive my brothers, sir," said Mort. "It is sir, isn't it, and not madam? Or miss? With you robots I'm never quite cert—"

"Of course I'm masculine," said Electro, briefly glancing down at himself. "I did get rid of any traces of Mother Z, didn't I?"

"I didn't mean to imply there was anything effeminate about you, sir," said Mort. "What I was trying to—"

"Mort's not much good at communicating with anyone," said Jerry. "You ought to see him trying to converse with an ape, or even a snerg. He actually has trouble getting through to tigers, if you can imagine that."

"Well, I don't fancy a tiger would be all that—"

"But we were raised by tigers," said Jerry. "Or rather Dad was. So there's a family tradition, as it were, for being able to get along with the things."

"Allow me," said Electro, "to introduce myself. I am Bozo the Robot and my young charges are Constance and Ulric Rowdybush, a devoted brother and sister I am escorting."

"Are you maybe lost in the jungle?" inquired both Mort and Jerry at once.

"No, we are perfectly aware of our location," replied Electro.

"Reason we ask," said Dik, "is we're pretty good at guiding lost travelers to safety. I mean, that is part of what jungle men do, after all."

"You still haven't," pointed out Jana while she and Tad approached the group, "told us who you are."

"Manners," said Jerry. "We're the Ty-Gor Triplets."

"Our father," added Dik, "was Ty-Gor."

"The famous jungle man," said Mort, watching their faces.

"Doesn't ring a bell, miss?"

"I bet she's heard of Ka-anga," said Jerry, kicking at a clump of moss with his big toe. "Him I bet she's heard of."

"Oh, yes, Ka-anga the jungle man," said Jana. "He was well-known when I was a child. He rescued lost travelers in the jungle, fought wild animals and occasionally stumbled onto a hidden civilization. Everybody's heard of him."

"He stole the whole idea from our dad," said Dik.

"Exactly," said Mort. "The entire jungle man gimmick was dreamed up by our father. He did it quite by accident, you understand. His parents were eaten by tharks and he was left alone in these wilds. Yes, alone in the wilderness, a wee babe of four years and—"

"Four years old, that's not so wee," said Jana.

"He was small for his age," said Jerry. "Now let me get on with the Ty-gor legend. Okay, so there was Pop a wee babe all alone and this maternal tiger found him and it chanced she had recently lost her own baby. She took in Dad and nursed him and reared him."

"That won't work, will it?" asked the girl. "You can't raise a human on tiger milk, can you?"

"Sure you can," said Dik. "She reared our Dad, didn't she?"

"Tiger's milk is good for you," said Mort.

"Anyhow, dad grew up with the tigers and he took to calling himself Ty-gor," continued Jerry. "See, it sounds sort of like tiger. Ty-gor."

"What was his real name?" Jana asked.

The brothers all studied their toes.

"It wasn't anything near so catchy," said Dik finally.

"No, Ty-gor has a real snappy quality. Ty-gor. Boy, with a name like that and the attack cry of the Bimoonda people Dad was—"

"What are the Bimoonda people?" Tad asked.

"Oh, just some people who yell frightening things when they attack their enemies."

"Do they live around here?"

"They used to," said Dik. "Ka-anga always claimed the tribe never existed and dad made up the yell. We, though, have the family scrapbooks up in the tree mansion and—"

"Do you live in a tree?" asked the girl.

"You have to," answered Dik. "It's part of the tradition. Jungle man, tree house. Of course, since there are three of us, we had to build bigger—"

"I'm certain you lads have other chores to attend to," put in Electro. "A jungle man's lot is a busy one, no doubt. We'll bid you a fond farewell,"

"Matter of fact," admitted Jerry, "you folks are the first lost travelers we've had in over a month."

"We sure would be pleased to guide you someplace," Dik offered, smiling hopefully at them.

"My own abilities as a guide are unexcelled," Electro told them. "Even though I didn't have the advantage of a parent who was suckled by a tiger."

"It's okay, you don't have to explain any further," said Jerry, his handsome face downcast.

"If you have nothing better to do," said Jana, "you can guide us for awhile. We're en route to the old URTS depot."

"Nix," the robot whispered in her ear, adding a gentle nudge in the ribs. "I don't want to confide our destination to anyone."

"We can trust the Ty-gor Triplets," she said. "Let them, Electro. It'll brighten their whole day."

After nearly a minute Electro said, "Lead on, gentlemen."

Chapter 21

"You've never known which way north it," Dik told Mort. "For a jungle man you have a piss poor sense of—"

"I know one thing, I know dad never went around using foul language in front of—"

"Gents," said Electro, addressing the halted trio. "We wish to take a leftwards direction at this forking of the trail. The entrance to the long abandoned underground railway facility should lie a scant half mile from us."

"But that path doesn't go north," said Dik.

"Yes, it does," Electro assured him. "Trust me, I have a built-in compass."

"One of the toughest things," Jerry said to Tad when they were moving along the new trail, "about being a jungle man is having to go barefoot. Even now, with my poor feet fairly calloused, I don't much enjoy it. Sometimes you step on a burr or prickers or a little spikey lizard and you let out a howl."

"Maybe you should," suggested Tad, "get into another line of work."

"Nope, that's impossible. Dad brought us up to be jungle men, it's in our blood. Dropping a tradition like the Ty-gor tradition isn't possible."

"Have you thought about wearing shoes?"

"Jungle men don't."

Jana was walking near the robot at the moment. "Why was this tunnel system we're heading for abandoned? Is it safe?"

"Perfectly safe and nearly in mint condition," replied Electro. "The Underground Rapid Transit System respresents a colossal boondoggle, my dear. Built near twenty years ago to enrich a gaggle of crooked local politicos. Oh, and there was some talk about bringing civilization to this part of the wilderness. Since no one in his or her right mind would want to inhabit this pesthole of a jungle, the system never thrived and soon fell into disuse."

"I wouldn't go so far as to characterize our jungle as a pesthole," said Dik.

"It is not a tourist's delight," said the robot. "You should be thankful URTS was a failure. Otherwise you'd be swinging from lamp posts instead of trees."

"Yes, but we'd have a lot more people passing through," said Mort. "One of the negative things about this jungle man trade is the tedium. Sit around and wait, sit around and wait."

"It wouldn't be boring if there were only one jungle man servicing the area," Dik pointed out.

"You couldn't handle it solo," Mort said. "You'd—"

"Allow me," said Electro, "to thank you for a most helpful piece of guidance." He made a sweeping gesture with his left arm. "We have arrived."

A relatively massive dome of multicolored glaz

stood before them. Each panel was three feet square and of a different pastel hue, the frame of the Underground Rapid Transit depot was of dark metal. Vines had long ago climbed high up the structure, flowering plants had followed. Birds perched on the tangle of branches, insects hid among the leaves humming.

"Doesn't give the impression of being a going concern," remarked Jana.

"There's a functional tubetram at this end of the line." Electro nodded across the high grass of the depot clearing. "I've been in touch with the dispatching computer while we've been on our hike. Fairly sensible old mechanism, except for a slight touch of amnesia. This tropical climate does it."

"I doubt there are," Dik was saying to Mort.

"We'd better check anyway, that's the Ty-gor style."

"What's he beefing about now?" inquired Jerry.

"We have to precede these folks into the depot," said Mort, pointing at the overgrown edifice. "To confront any perils which might be lurking within."

His jungle man brother studied the building as they all came downhill toward it. "We're not noted for indoor work."

"Wasn't Dad always stumbling on some lost city or other?"

"This isn't a lost city, it's a lost subway terminal," said Jerry. "For that matter, it isn't really very lost since everybody seems to know it's here."

"We're quite capable of fending for ourselves from here onward," said Electro.

"Notice the windows are covered with vegetation and dirt," said Mort. "Making for gloomy conditions inside, a perfect place for trouble to be lurking."

The metal and glaz doorway was twenty feet wide and equally high. Its once-handsome metal and glaz doors were sprung from their hinges and hung at broken-wing angles.

"Think there really might be trouble in there?" Tad asked the girl.

"Rodents or snakes maybe."

"The dispatcher assured me there are no major hazards, though his memory problem may have kept him from telling me all." The robot strode toward the shadowy threshold.

Mort went sprinting past him. "Me first. Better let a Ty-gor check things out." He bounded inside and was lost to view.

The robot remained on the edge of entering.

"At last, at last! Our prayers have been answered! O, praise St. Reptillicus and the blessed bones—"

"Less religious fervor and more action!"

"Oof!"

Several old and quavery voices could be heard inside the old depot dome, along with the sounds of a scuffle.

"Wouldn't you know it? The first mark in months and he doesn't even have any pockets."

Pink!

Electro had snapped his fingers. "That must be what the dimwitted computer was trying to remember," he said. "Muggers."

"You think Mort is being set upon by a gang of muggers?" asked Jerry.

Electro took a step into the interior. "Approximately a dozen of them are—"

"Bangalla! Bangalla!"

"Bangalla! Bangalla!"

The remaining Ty-gors ran inside.

"Should we help?" Tad joined the robot, trying to see what was going on inside the dimly lit URT depot.

Dust was rising in the far right corner of the murky

place. Tad could make out, in the thin stripes of tinted sunlight which made it through the dome, a gang of lizard men, catmen and humans swarming over the triplets.

"Observe more carefully," advised Electro.

Tad did. "Hey, those muggers are all old men."

"Ancient. They must be the original muggers, here since the depot opened two decades ago."

"They're wearing out," Tad said. "Listen to the way some of them are wheezing. It's sad."

"The one with the wheeze is Mort," said Electro. "No doubt he has a few allergies, and the jungle is a bad place to live when you suffer with—"

"Bangalla! Bangalla!" Dik was placing a foot atop a mound of fallen old muggers, beating his broad chest.

"That was the Ty-gor triumphal shout," Jerry called to them through cupped hands.

"Very close to the attack yell," Electro called back. "The inflections are slightly different."

"Can I come in now?" Jana was beside Tad, linking her arm in his.

"The Ty-gor brothers have overcome all the muggers."

"That's as it should be." Arm in arm, they crossed the weedy plaz-square floor of the depot to the site of the recent brawl.

"I didn't get a good look at these fellows while we were subduing them." Dik was squatting beside a pile of uncounscious muggers, frowning into the sunlit face of the top man. This was a human type with a white beard of admirable length. "What I'm getting at is, this one at least gives every indication of being around eighty years old."

"There's no forced retirement in the villainy field," said Mort, striving to catch his breath.

"Still, I feel somewhat of a ninny and a simp," said Dik while he got down on hands and knees to inspect a mugger lower in the stack, "giving off the triumphal cry over a bunch of senior citizens."

Jerry was circling another pile of knocked out muggers. "The one on the bottom here may well be a little old lady of ninety," he said. "This is getting embarrassing."

Electro said, "Why don't you lads quickly slip away into the jungle. This little incident we'll keep to ourselves."

"This catman isn't even breathing," said Jerry, ignoring the robot's suggestion. "I'd best tug him out of the stack and . . . oops! Now I've dislodged his hearing aid."

"Gentlemen, I'm a qualified paramedic." Electro eased Jerry aside and extracted the catman from the unconscious group. "This old chap isn't dead, merely in a coma. You three scamper back to the brooks and fens of your beloved jungle. I'll administer medical care to these poor unfortunates and slip them a little remedial therapy as well. Guide them toward new and more fulfilling careers."

"Let's take the robot up on his offer, fellas," said Mort. "The fetid air in this place is getting to my sinuses. And I think that old lady must have whacked me a good one in the groin with her walking stick."

"I suppose that wouldn't be inconsistent with the code of the Ty-gors."

"Not at all," Jana assured them.

"Well, then," said Dik, "we'll bid you farewell."

"So long," said Tad. "Bangalla to you all."

"Bangalla!" The triplets, with Mort in the middle, went strolling away.

"Now to business," said Electro.

Chapter 22

"I don't see the hat as necessary," remarked Tad.

"A perfectly legitimate piece of headgear, my boy." Electro gave the striped engineer cap a pat, returned both hands to the controls of the underground tram.

They were shooting along the tunnel trax at the rate of a hundred miles an hour. It had taken Electro only a few minutes to get the three-car tram into working order.

"How are we going to get my father and the rest out of the plantation?" Tad asked.

"We'll work out the final plan when we're on the scene. At this very moment I'm in communication with a reliable computer on the plantation grounds, collecting data."

"According to this," said Jana, holding up a faded brochure she'd found on one of the wicker seats, "we'll emerge less than fifty miles from the Blackwatch plantation."

"Forty-seven miles," said Electro. "At the rate we're traveling we ought to reach there by early after—"

Crunch! Krunk!

Their tram car hopped, shook and groaned. It slowed, hopped, stopped dead.

"It's the same thing every time I ride this nerfing train!" complained an old voice from the other end of the car.

"You haven't ridden this in nineteen years, Leslie."

"True, Royston, but when last I did the nerfing thing stopped right about here. And you may recall what a night that was, the night of the Monumental Blizzard."

"There's another thing I object to," said Tad. "Giving a lift to those three supposedly reformed muggers."

"It's the least we could do," said Electro, "since the Ty-gor family maimed them and rendered them incapable of further criminal activities."

"Conductor, what's the matter?" hollered Leslie, an ancient catman.

"Nothing serious." Electro left the controls, trotted to an emergency door. "I have but to reconnect our roof cable."

"Ha, that'll be some fun," said Leslie. "I remember the night of the Colossal Ceiling Leaks when old Mel the conductor attempted that and the snakes got him."

"That wasn't the night of the Colossal Ceiling Leaks," commented Royston, a bearded human of eighty-six. "It was the afternoon of the Vandalized Windows. Old Mel left the car and six huge vipers jumped him."

"Quite a sight," chuckled the third passenger, a dappled old lizard man.

Electro was fiddling with the emergency door. "Interesting how this thing refuses to open."

"Says you have to open that panel there with a coin," Tad pointed out.

"Folderol, my boy. Those instructions are for halfwits like our load of muggers. There's no lock in the universe I can't pick."

"Exactly what Mel the conductor said before the snakes got him."

Jana said, "Why not use a coin, Electro? This tunnel is not a very cheery place to be stuck."

"We were stuck here once for three days and two nights," said old Leslie. "That was the week of the Devastating Flood. Trapped down here with the water rising up as high as—"

"There's no valid reason I can't persuade this fool door to open." Electro had been trying various fingers and the gadgets therein on the lock mechanism.

"Why don't you open this panel with a coin?" asked Tad.

"All right, my boy, we'll do it the halfwit way." Electro ran a metal finger along the instructions lettered on the panel next to the emergency door. "How To Open Door In Case Of Emergency. One. Summon conductor. Two. Call on St. Reptillicus for guidance . . . an unnecessary mixing of religion with civic life. Three. Insert a coin in this slot to unlock this panel. Four. Coin must be a ten centime double caribou piece with the royal caribou on the obverse and Bonnie Prince Harlan on the reverse. Indeed? And where, short of a rare coin dealer, does one come upon a—"

"I've got a whole pocket full of the nerfing things," called Leslie, standing up and jiggling. "We rolled a numismatist some months back." He managed to extract one from his pocket and toss it the length of the car to the robot.

"Much obliged."

"Anything we can do to help," said Royston. "After all, you rehabilitated us and are taking us back to civilization where we can trod the straight and narrow once again."

Stooping slightly, Electro used the coin.

Ponk!

The panel popped out.

More instructions were printed within the cabinet the panel revealed.

1. Congratulations! You have successfully completed the first step of the emergency exit process.

2. Pause and give thanks to St. Serpentine.

3. Insert a coin in the slot marked A (B in some trams).

4. Coin must be the charming little five rupee piece with the profile of King Earl the Tipsy on its face.

"Nertz," observed Electro, insterting his little finger into the slot.

Zzurp! Ziztle!

The emergency door sizzled for several seconds, then slid open.

"Was that a snake I heard?" asked Leslie.

Electro jumped out of the tram. "Have it fixed in a jiffy."

"Don't step on any snakes," said Jana.

"There are no snakes out here." Electro moved to the front of the car. "Even if there were, I'm impervious."

Tad walked to the head of the tram to watch Electro climb up the ladder on the nose of the car. "I hope he can get us rolling again soon."

Jana said, "Yes, so do I."

"You sound less than enthusiastic. Getting to Blackwatch, saving everybody . . . that's what we set out to do. We're getting fairly close."

"Once we reach the place and once we succeed," said the girl, "then everything will change."

"Sure, but for the better."

"I don't know," she said.

Chapter 23

"No, that's not an ominous sound," decided Electro, a hand cupped to his ear.

"It's a guitar," said Tad. "After what happened to you on the showboat we—"

"Someone inside this inn is in a festive mood, playing the guitar and singing agricultural ditties." The robot gestured at the oaken door of the inn across the dark courtyard.

"This is probably a safe place to stop," Jana said. "We have been walking all afternoon."

Tad frowned at the sign over the doorway. "Not a cozy name, the Manacle & Fetter."

"Name no doubt derives from the inn's proximity to the Blackwatch Plantation, my boy. It's a good spot to pick up gossip about conditions inside the plantation."

"You're already in contact with a computer at the place."

"We could use some human information," Electro

told him. "In planning an assault, the more information the better."

They crossed the night courtyard and, Electro first, entered the main room of the Manacle & Fetter.

It was a dining room, nearly empty. In a corner near the blazing fireplace four people were gathered around a large table. Three of them sat watching the fourth, a frail catman who was strumming on a battered guitar and singing.

"Oh, the weevils ate my cotton
And the snergs carried off my maze!
Yes, them weevils ate all my cotton
And the snergs they . . ."

"Good evening, madam," said the plump lizard proprietor, hurrying up to Electro. "Would you mind going tiptoe to your table?"

"Is that the custom in these parts?" Electro was disguised as a middle-aged catwoman.

"It's on account of the recording session." Proceeding on his toes, he led them to a table on the opposite side of the dining room. "That's the entire Primitive And Lowdown Music Department from Esmeralda University."

"Fancy that," said Electro as the innkeeper pulled out his chair for him.

"Oh, the tharks chased off my grout herd
And the chiggers ate my wife.
Yes, them tharks they . . ."

Tad, who along with the girl was made up as a catperson, took a seat at the round table. "He's worse than Mother Zarzarkas."

"I don't know," said the robot, glancing at the rural singer. "There's a certain—"

Thong!

"Doggone, there went another dang one." A string had broken on the catman's guitar. He shook his furry head in dismay.

"Why did you show up with such a tacky guitar, Goody? I keep telling you—"

"Why should he have a new guitar? He's a shit kicker, not some slick—"

"You can only carry authenticity so far, Marcia. I am fairly damn tired of his guitar breaking every five—"

"We want a certain sound, Harvey. We want a raw, earthy, gutsy—"

"He can be raw and earthy without breaking a damn string every five—"

"Please, please," said the large bearded man who was the oldest in the group. "We must have less quibbling and more singing. Restring your instrument, Goody. Shame on you, Marcia. Shame on you, Harvey."

"I'm not charmed by this whole evening, Dr. Brattle," said Harvey Conn-Hedison, a blue-feathered birdman. "Things began going wrong when we left Potato Center and I had to ride backwards in the Rolling Folkmobile. Then when Marcia insisted we stop so she could proposition that crossing sweeper in—"

"I sensed that big, exciting, muscle-loaded darling was a folk singer," said Marcia Fork, an overweight catwoman of forty. "You have to have an instinct for—"

"I admit he was able to warble a work song while keeping time with his push broom, Marcia. You know darn well, however, that—"

"Got her restrung, folks," announced Goody Waggoner. "Speaking of potatoes, would you like me to do my song about how the potato bugs they got into my—"

"We already have sufficient potato songs, thank you, Goody," Dr. Brattle told him.

"Too many," said Harvey. "Since Marcia was trying to vamp that potato sacker with the nine-string guitar, we ended up with—"

"The fact that he was a stunning, limber, broad-shouldered devil had nothing to do with it," said Marcia. "He knew nineteen fresh and new songs about potatoes, exactly the sort of thing the Rolling Folkmobile is supposed to be gathering." She patted one of their recording boxes with her paw.

"A little cool-headed research, done without the benefit of hot pants, Marcia, is going to show that most of his potato ballads were created simply by substituting the word potato for other words in common everyday old songs," said the angry Harvey. "For example, his 'Let's Go Frig O'Riley's Potato' is a rather simple-minded swipe of—"

"Please, please, we must finish up with Goody," reminded Dr. Brattle. "Otherwise we'll reach the Blackwatch Plantation after they close the gates for the night."

"And how about 'I Got The Longest Potato In The Navy'? I suppose it hasn't occured to you that—"

"Oh, ho!" Electro beamed at Tad and the girl. "This may be what we're seeking."

Tad, in a low voice, said, "A way to get inside the plantation."

"Exactly," said the robot. "Yonder academics obviously have access to Blackwatch Plantation. No doubt to record the off-key wailing of some wretched prisoner."

"So if we," said Jana, "can take their places we'll be able to slip in there."

Electro shifted in his chair, raising his voice. "Excuse me," he said toward the music scholars. "I couldn't help overhearing your conversation. Since we are all intensely interested in the folk idiom I thought perhaps. . . ."

Chapter 24

Stroking his beard, Electro scanned the packet of faxforms and permits. "It appears we're scheduled to record a . . . left turn here, my boy."

"I'm trying to turn left," Tad told him. "It's tricky with feathers all over my hands and arms."

"You make a highly believable birdman," said the robot. "The officials at Blackwatch Plantation will accept you without batting an eye."

"I ought to look like Harvey Conn-Hedison, I'm decked out in his feathers." Tad got their Rolling Folkmobile onto the roadway leading through the night to the plantation.

"We plucked the poor chap rather rapidly, I think. The appointment is for ten and we should make that with ease. When your cousin built a plucking device into me I little dreamed—"

"Who is it we're supposed to be recording?" Jana was in the guise of the plump catwoman now.

"Ah, yes." Electro returned to the papers he'd acquired from the stunned Dr. Brattle. "We are to capture on record the field hollers and work blues of a fellow known as Hamfixin, sent here by disgruntled neighbors and relatives. Seems every time Hamfixin, who is by way of being a habitual murderer, was brought to trial he performed one of his tunes for judge and jury and brought tears to their eyes. After a long and annoying series of acquittals his contemporaries took extra-legal steps and had him railroaded into Blackwatch. Causing, by the way, real estate values in his old neighborhood to soar."

"Has Hamfixin seen Dr. Brattle before?" Tad was watching the dark road they were traveling along.

"This is to be his maiden encounter with the Department of Primitive And Lowdown Music. We'll have no trouble passing muster," Electro assured him. "The officials and guards have never laid eyes on the real Brattle and his crew before, either."

"Do you," asked Jana, "know the layout of the plantation?"

"My computer contact has provided me with detailed diagrams. Here, I'll run one off for you." He hummed, lifted his left buttock and extracted a map from a slot therein.

Taking the document, Jana studied it. "High thick walls all around, forest and mountains to the rear. Guard towers at . . . six, seven, eight . . . at eight positions around the wall. Each turret manned by a pair of robots and a set of blaster cannons."

"Blackwatch is one of the more secure lockups in the territory," said Electro.

"Where exactly is my father?" Tad asked.

"My contact doesn't have that information. It is safe, however, to conjecture he's in one of the five barracks compounds near the East wall. I've marked those with an X in red."

"This X is purple," said Jana.

Electro thumped his side. "Been having a bit of trouble with my inking gear since I revived. Purple, then."

"What about my father?" asked the girl.

"I assume he, too, my dear, is in one of the barracks. Which one, we will have to determine when we arrive. Cousin Cosmo, Tad, will be in one of those five barracks and his dear wife, Alice, should be ensconced in one of the female barracks compounds, which are marked with a blue X."

"Green," corrected Jana. "There on the west side of the plantation, next to the warehouses and loading areas."

"We may have to spring people from four separate spots, then," said Tad.

"Once inside the walls I'll find some way to get into the administration building and have a go at the chief computer. Find out where everyone is stored."

Tad rubbed at his nose, twice. "What exactly do they grow at Blackwatch?"

"Drive especially carefully from here," advised Electro. "My indicators show there's a fairly heavy trace of it in the air now we're nearly there."

"A good deal of what?"

"Dreamdust," said Electro.

"Dreamdust? That's a hallucinatory pollen, isn't it? It's supposed to be illegal on this planet," said Tad.

"To your dear Cousin Joshua and his cohorts very little is illegal, my boy. Which is why they can operate Blackwatch and grow this stuff," said the robot. "You'll notice on the map that over three hundred acres are given over to the cultivation of dreamdust bushes."

"Hey!" Tad smacked the brake button with his open palm.

Several small children were playing in the road, oblivious of the approaching landvan.

"Keep going," said Electro.

"I can't run over those kids."

"There's nothing in the road," the robot said. "You're having a mild hallucination from the dreamdust in the air."

"He's right, Tad," said Jana. "I don't see any kids. Just be careful not to run into any of those grazing shugs."

"There are no shugs either, my dear." Electro turned in his seat to pat the girl on the knee with a metal hand.

Tad shook his head, started the van moving ahead. The children faded as they approached. "This is going to be a handicap, not being able to tell what's real."

"A dilemma which has given pause to many a philosopher." He lifted up his left hand. The tip of his thumb popped open and a small needle rose up. "I'd best give you both injections to counteract the dust. Won't hurt a bit."

"Ouch," said Tad when the needle found his flesh.

"Sorry, I'm not used to inoculating feathered patients. You next, Jana."

In less than five minutes they were pulling up before the high stone walls of the Blackwatch Plantation. Thick solid metal gates kept them out.

Globes of light came floating down from the towers on each side of the gates—a dozen globes, which came to hover over the landvan, shedding an intense yellow glow onto the Rolling Folkmobile and its occupants.

"Nature of business?" The inquiring voice came from one of the towers and was vastly amplified.

Electro pushed his disguised head out into the night. "Yes, yes, you're expecting us and there's no need for all this fuss," he said. "I'm Dr. Martin G. Brattle, head of the Department of Primitive and Lowdown Music at Esmeralda University."

"Throw your permits and passes to the left of your vehicle."

"At least they didn't ask for a ten *centime* piece," said Jana while Electro passed the documents to Tad to toss out.

The packet had barely settled in the dusty road when a sharp-nosed missile came whistling down from the right-hand tower. It circled low over the flung papers, seemed to be taking pictures and sniffing.

"Relatively unsophisticated scanning bug," remarked Electro.

"Papers are in order. You will proceed onto the plantation grounds. You will stop on the yellow section of parking area in front of the Administration Building. Do not leave your vehicle until told to. Doing so will result in harm to your person."

Tad cleared his throat, tensed.

The gates, silently, swung open.

The landvan went rolling inside, the globes of light following.

As the van stopped on the designated area a door in the squat white stone Administration Building opened. Five men came out to stand on the broad stone staircase and watch the arrival.

"Could I still be having hallucinations?" Tad asked the robot.

"Unlikely. Why?"

"Because I see Hohl, the overseer from Foghill, standing over there."

Electro nodded. "Be calm, it is he. The lout has no reason to suspect us, our disguises are nigh perfect."

"Let's hope the same goes for my husband," said Jana.

Tad asked, "Your husband?"

"That's him on the second step from the top," she said.

Chapter 25

"He's sort of old," said Tad.

Jana's husband was a tall man, lean and not handsome. He was in his middle thirties, with thinning dark hair and wearing a gray cloak.

"Older than me. I already told you that."

"Nitwit," muttered Electro.

"Me?"

"Talking about my computer contact," said the robot. "He neglected to tell me Hohl and Taine had shown up here at Blackwatch."

"They may tumble to us."

"Admittedly they are here in anticipation of our arrival," said Electro, "since they've obviously figured out where it is we've been aiming for. However, I'm confident our mutual gift for mimicry will serve . . . here we go."

A chubby man in a nubby cloak had detached himself from the stairway group and was coming across the yellow flagstone to their landvan. "This is a real honor," he said, chuckling. "I'm Supervisor Bunner, in charge of the entire plantation . . . Look out for that seagull!" He ducked quickly, swatting at the night air.

"Dreamdust," muttered Electro.

"Please step out of your van, friends," invited Bunner. "I can't tell you how pleased I am to greet visitors of your standing. Dr. Brattle, I've poured over your books and lecturdiscs. You are, sir, a brilliant, brilliant man. I must remark, though, you don't look in person as you do on your pixdiscs."

Climbing out of the cab, Electro said, "Electronic distortion. I'm often told I look smaller and less plump on the screen."

"I've read every one of your books, we have them in the library here. And since the library is off limits to all the miserable wretches who work on the plantation the books are all in really nice shape." He shook his plump head from side to side. "I have to admit I'm awful at remembering titles. What was the name of that book of yours I liked so much?"

Electro said, "Like most of my readers you probably enjoyed *Sea Chanties: Form And Function.*"

The supervisor blinked. "Why, I don't remember that title at all."

Jana eased out of the landvan. "He must be thinking of *Folk Songs, Work Songs And The Growth Of The Barnum Hegemony,* doctor."

"Yes, that's it." Bunner clapped his hands together. "I can't express how much pleasure that book gave me. You see, I love to read in bed and since I've had my chambers sound-proofed so I can't hear the pitiful moans and groans of our field hands I'm able to read a good deal more than previously. What are the titles of some of your other books, Dr. Brattle?"

"The favorites," supplied Jana, "are usually *Blues*

Songs, Yodels, Random Whistling And Man's Fate, Murder Ballads And The Development Of Intergalactic Trade and *Polkas: Interaction And Transcendence.*"

"Yes, exactly. I've read every one of those, doctor, and was simply ravaged by your intellect."

"Most people are," acknowledged Electro. "Now if you would be so kind as to escort us to Mr. Hamfixin."

Tad had left the cab and moved carefully around to Jana's side. "How'd you know those titles?"

"I'm well-read," she answered into his ear.

Tad turned to the robot. "We're behind schedule, doctor. We're never going to gather enough mat—"

"Who's that knock-kneed mooncalf? I know that dopey walk!" Hohl left the Administration Building steps to come bounding toward them.

"Here, here, Mr. Hohl," cautioned the supervisor. "I won't have you threatening people of the standing of Dr. Brattle or—"

"Stow it in your gooz, lardbutt!" Hohl halted a few feet from Tad, scrutinizing him through narrowed eyes. "Birdman, huh? You're a pretty snerfy looking birdman. Those feathers look like plaz to me."

"Who is this oaf?" Tad asked the supervisior in what he hoped was a fair imitation of Harvey Conn-Hedison's voice. "Really, Supervisor Bunner, we wouldn't have come all this way to your ragtag plantation had we known we'd be assaulted by oafish—"

"I'll assault your biffy, you slurpnosed goober!" Hohl raised a fist, shook it.

"Mr. Hohl, please." The supervisor, blushing, grabbed his arm and tugged him back from Tad. "I'll thank you to leave my guests alone."

"You scatter-brain!" bellowed Hohl. "Aren't we

here because we figure Electro and Tad Rhymer and that beanpole snerd's sleep-around wife are due here any minute? Then in pops a big guy and a wimpy guy and a bimbo who—"

"I've viewed many a canned lecture by the doctor, Hohl! I'd know him anywhere, once I take the electronic distortion factor into consideration. They'll be no further chatter about this matter in front of my respected guests."

"Somebody's going to distort your gob if . . . Oh, dear. Have I been ranting like an utter fool again?" Hohl pressed a hand to his face, massaging his cheeks. "It's my darned old allergies again, plus the nerfing dreamdust in the air. I sincerely apologize to one and all."

"Well you should." Supervisor Bunner brushed at Hohl's shoulders. "Shoo those seagulls off yourself, too, they're very unsightly."

"Ahum," put in Electro. "May we begin our interview with Mr. Hamfixin? I'm planning an entire chapter in my forthcoming book about this little jaunt. Of course, Mr. Bunner, you'll figure prominently in the text and several laudatory footnotes."

"I've always treated Hamfixin well, insisted to the guards that they never break too many of his fingers at one time." Bunner chuckled. "Gather up your equipment and I'll escort you to the little maximum security cottage where we have Hamfixin stashed."

"This is altogether fascinating." Hohl watched Tad lift a recording box from out of the landvan. "I'd like to observe your recording session."

"You may tag along," said the supervisor, "only if you promise not to shout and hit at people."

"Heaven fordid," said Hohl. "It's only my unfortunate allergies which cause such unhappy outburts, and I feel I've got them under control again."

"You won't mind if Mr. Hohl accompanies us, Dr. Brattle?"

"Well, one tries to keep all unsettling elements out of a recording session," said the robot.

"I won't unsettle anybody," promised Hohl.

Electro shrugged, hesitating. "Very well," he said finally. "You may join in the fun, sir."

"I hope one more observer won't give you trouble, doctor," said the lean man in the gray cloak who was walking their way.

"What do you say, doctor? I know Mr. Taine is a student and admirer of folk music."

"Yes, I certainly am," said Jana's husband in his harsh, nasal voice.

Electro had obviously made a decision. "Come one, come all," he invited. "This bids fair to be a memorable evening."

Chapter 26

"Shoo! Scram!" Supervisor Bunner swatted at the night. "It's a shame the way these seagulls plague us. So far inland, too."

Jana's husband had chosen to walk beside Tad across the plantation grounds. "A very interesting field you're in, Mr. Conn-Hedison."

"Many people don't see it that way at all."

"My own collection of primitive music of this planet is quite extensive," said Taine. "My late wife wasn't as fond of simple—"

"Your wife is dead?" asked Tad.

"Excuse me, a slip of the tongue. I tend to think of her as such, although as yet. . . . But no need to burden you with my domestic problems."

They passed the enormous stone warehouse, three giant buildings ringed by parked landvans. There was a strong musky smell in the night air, caused probably by the dreamdust pollen. The maximum security cottage was apparently nowhere near the men's barracks buildings. Tad had expected to feel anxious and excited, now he was this close to his father. Instead he was extremely calm, feeling almost numb.

". . . your favorite?" Taine was asking him.

Tad coughed into his feathery hand. "Difficult to say." A feather left his hand, went spinning away.

"In other words you feel—"

"Growl! Wow!"

Thunka! Thum!

Supervisor Bunner raised a cautionary hand, stopping. They were a few yards from a low stone building with heavy metal doors and barred windows. "He may be in one of his moods," he told Electro.

"Feeling murderous, is he?"

"Gruff! Woop!"

Smop!

"I suppose you can't record Hamfixin if he's in a restraining coat?"

"Be difficult for him to pick his guitar."

Bunner's chubby chin went up and down. "Yes, I can understand that. How about if some of my guards sit on him?"

"That, too, would be inhibiting."

"Let's bust in there and stomp the nerfing bastard!" suggested Hohl. "Let's take his frapping banjo and stuff it in his bafflebar!"

"He doesn't play a banjo," said Electro, scratching at his beard.

"Whatever he plays, let's jam it in—"

"Perhaps, Supervisor Bunner," continued Electro, "we'd best postpone our visit until morning. By then Mr. Hamfixin may be in a calmer mood."

"Hard to predict," said the supervisor. "These homicidal rages of his sometimes drag on for days." He sighed. "Perhaps I shouldn't have let him read the recording contract you people sent. I really fear that's what has set him off this time."

"Grop! Wowsie! Twenty-five percent of offplanet sales!"

Thabom!

"When he gets to throwing the guards around," said Bunner, "it usually indicates he's very upset."

"You're losing feathers," said Jana, close to Tad.

"Only a few. Most bird people do."

"Be careful. Don't bounce or wiggle any more than necessary."

"Wasn't planning to."

Bunner ventured up to the cottage door. "Let me try a few standard subduing tactics," he said, placing an eye to the spyhole in the door. "My, six guards out cold and three more woozy." From somewhere within his cloak he took a copper rod. "This gas, though not always, has a calming effect on him."

"He's of no use to us if he's too subdued," said Electro.

"We'll hope for a satisfactory mean between crazed violence and doddering docility." Bunner twisted the end of the rod and a yellowish mist went whispering into the cottage through the spyhole.

"Fifty percent of *net!* Growr!"

Tink!

"Ah, he's not throwing them as far," said Bunner, chuckling. "I do believe we're making progress."

A full minute went by with no further indication of violence from within the cottage.

Electro peered into the spyhole. "He's plopped down in a chair, tuning his guitar."

"Splendid." The supervisor pulled out a multikey and inserted it into the multilock on the thick door.

Tad, after a quick glance at Taine, put an arm

around Jana's shoulders. "Hold back until we're sure it's safe."

"Good evening, Hamfixin." Bunner took a few steps into the place.

"Evenin to yer," said the large black man seated in the synskin chair with a twelve string-guitar resting on his knee.

Four guards were still standing, several more were strewn on the padded floor or draped over the simple furniture.

"Done been thinkin," said Hamfixin, huge fingers resting on the guitar strings. "Been done thinkin bout how I uster work on that cabbage farm when I weren't no more higher than a snerg's belly button an one day my old mam done—"

"Whoa," said Electro. "We should be catching all this. Could you curb your recollections till we have our equipment set up, Mr. Hamfixin?"

"Who are this whiskery joker?" the singer asked Bunner.

"Why, this is Dr. Martin G. Brattle, come all this way to record you and your marvelous music."

"Ugly motherfuyer, ain't he? Remind me of a joker I done killed back when I was picking garbanzos down in the delta country round—"

"Save the memoirs until my associate is ready for you. Harvey, let's get cracking."

"Yes, at once." Tad left Jana, came into the room and placed the recording box on the floor near Hamfixin's chair.

"Who am this dude with all the plumage?"

"I'm Harvey Conn-Hedison, Dr. Brattle's devoted aid."

"Asswarmer," said Hamfixin. "You know, I done been all over this planet an I been down so low sometime as I hadder look up at—"

"Are we getting this now, Harvey?"

"Everything is functioning, doctor."

"Good, good. Then you can go ahead, Mr. Hamfixin." Electro circled the room until he was close to Tad. He whispered, "When all these nitwits are in here I'll stun the lot. Then we hightail it for the Ad Building."

"I'm ready." He turned to summon Jana in from outside and noticed she was talking to her husband. "Marcia, can you get over here, please."

"Yes, of course, Harvey." The girl entered, came to Tad. "What?"

"How come you're talking to—"

"I couldn't very well avoid it without making everybody suspicious."

"When everyone's in here, Electro'll stun them. Then we move."

"Okay." She returned to the doorway. "Do come in, Mr. Taine. You too, Mr. Hohl."

"The door ought to be shut," said Bunner. "You do have a tendency to escape, Hamfixin. You're quite footloose."

"I is as footloose as a snickerbug hoppin on a—"

"Suppose you start with one of your blues tunes?" Electro, once Hohl and Taine were inside, shut the heavy door. He remained with his back to it.

"You alls the time is talkin over my talkin, motherhumper," said Hamfixin. "Got me in mind of a joker I cut up whiles I was plucking dummler beans on a plantation long ways from here. That was when I done made up my 'Nineteen Sacks A Day Quota Or They Gone Bust Your Ass Blues.' I believes I do that one right now." The fingers of his left hand pressed down on the strings, his right hand commenced strumming. "Woke up this morning with them ol dummler bean bugs nibblin on my—"

"Could you wait a second, Mr. Hamfixin," said Electro. "I'm not absolutely certain our recording box is working. Harvey, cart it over here. You come have a look as well, Marcia."

Tad was bending for the box when Hamfixin leaped from his chair.

"Growr!" cried the black man. "It ain't bad enough you interrupt my bio, it ain't bad enough you step on my patter . . . you got to interrupt my musical narratives also! I gonna kill you, you ugly motherfuyer! Gonna kill you graveyard dead!" He flung aside his guitar.

The instrument whacked Tad across the bridge of the nose before continuing across the room to land among fallen guards.

"Temper, temper," warned the supervisor, reaching for his superduing rod once more.

"Gonna pull them ugly whiskers out by they roots!" Hamfixin lunged at Electro.

The robot was swinging up a hand. "I have to warn you that—"

"Never did done like a man with facefuzz since the time . . . well, I'll be dipped!" Hamfixin stumbled back from Electro, glancing from the robot's exposed metal chin to the full beard he was clutching in his hand.

"The robot!" bellowed Hohl. "It's the nerfing robot!"

Chapter 27

"Then it's obvious who *you* must be!" Taine lunged for Jana.

All at once there was nothing else in the room except that charging figure. "You aren't going to hurt her!" Tad tackled the girl's husband.

Taine swung down with both fists clasped, striking Tad hard against the side of his head. "So you're the one. The bastard she ran off with this time."

Tad held on, succeeded in pitching Taine over onto the padded floor. He let go, dived for the lean man's torso. He got one hand around Taine's throat, struck at him with the other.

Taine twisted, brought his knees up into Tad's groin. "She won't stay. She'll run. She always does."

"Shut up! Just shut up!" He jabbed his fist into Taine's face. Twice, three times. Again.

Finally, he realized the man was unconscious beneath him. He took a deep breath, lifted up and away from him.

"Look out!" warned Jana's voice.

Tad spun, saw Hohl hurtling at him.

"Feathered little freak!" shouted the overseer. "I'll stomp your nerfing head into—"

"Not yet." Pivoting, Tad dodged the charge. He drove a fist into the passing Hohl's stomach.

"Foul me, will you? A man with multiple allergies!" Hohl growled, leaping for Tad.

This time he couldn't dodge.

Hohl's body hit him and they both slammed back into the wall. "Teach you to skip out!" He pummeled Tad with both fists.

"I don't like you, Hohl," said Tad, feeling the remark wasn't quite strong enough. He struggled to avoid the overseer's blows. But it was impossible. The air was being slammed out of him, pain was zigzagging through his body.

Zzizle!

"Yow!" Hohl screamed, brought both hands up to the sides of his head.

Zzang!

Hohl howled. Danced back away from Tad. Tripped over someone, fell backwards. Let go his head, flapped his arms. Dropped unconscious, flat on his back. Next to the unconscious form of Supervisor Bunner.

Tad held onto the wall with one hand. "Thanks."

"If you persist in fighting fair, my boy, you're going to continue to have difficulties." Electro stood in the center of the room, casually rubbing the tips of his metal fingers together. "Although you didn't handle things too badly."

Only Tad and the robot and Jana remained upright. Everyone else was distributed somewhere on the floor of the maximum security cottage. The guards,

Supervisor Bunner, Jana's husband, Hohl and even Hamfixin.

"I lost track of what was going on," said Tad, still bracing himself against the wall. "When I saw Taine going for you, Jana, I—"

"Yes, I know. I saw." She wended her way through the stunned bodies to him.

"Very old-fashioned approach you have, my boy, very organic," remarked Electro. "But then you don't come equipped with stunguns, subduing mist and—"

"We aren't going to have much time," Tad cut in. "We better get to the Administration Building."

"You're absolutely right." Electro stepped over a sprawled guard, rolled over another and stooped. He retrieved his beard, slapped it back on his face. "Hardly as convincing as it might be, but I trust sufficient to get by on a dark night."

"You haven't lost too many feathers," Jana told Tad, putting an arm around him. "Let me help you walk.

He shook his head, which made his new headache worse. "I'm going to have to walk into that place unaided, otherwise it'll make people suspicious."

Electro, avoiding the scattered bodies as much as possible, tromped to the door and opened it a fraction. "Apparently everyone is used to sounds of violence from this joint. No one is lurking outside. Shall we depart?"

"Yeah, let's go." Tad moved free of the girl, managed to walk across the room and out into the night.

"A most sentimental man, your Supervisor Bunner," Electro was saying to the two guards and the assistant supervisor who stood on the stone steps of the Administration Building.

"What do you mean, Dr. Brattle?" asked the assistant supervisor, a small near-sighted lizard man.

"I mean the fellow insisted on remaining in Hamfixin's cottage while the singer ran through his entire repertoire of ditties about mother and fireside. Extremely touching."

"Meantime," said Tad, "he told us we might use his office to go over the material we've recorded."

"Yes, I suppose that's all right."

"Fishy," commented one of the guards.

"Fishy," echoed the other guard.

Electro, very gingerly, stroked his beard and gazed at the two burly catmen. "Are you hinting at some lack of truth in my account of Mr. Bunner's nocturnal activities?"

"Sounds like so much bushwah," said one guard.

"Lot of horsepuckey," added the other.

"Unfortunate." Electro raised the middle finger of his right hand. A line of pale orange light shot out of it, hitting the chest of first one guard and then the other.

While they were dropping to their knees the beam touched the assistant supervisor and he, too, toppled.

"When verbal stratagems fail, my boy, resort to gadgets." Electro frisked the keys off one of the guards, unlocked the doors. "Assist me in dragging these skeptics inside and out of sight."

Chapter 28

"We can bring this off with a distinct flourish," announced Electro. He stood in the center of the control room, arms spread wide. "Yes, a flourish is what is called for."

Two of the large room's walls were covered with monitor screens which showed sections of the plantation grounds as well as the interiors of the barracks and warehouses.

Tad was at a row of data boxes. "Here's what we want," he said, easing a faxprint out of a box slot. "This thing just printed the locations of everyone we want. My father is in Barracks B, Cousin Cosmo is in C, Cousin Alice is in E and, Jana, your dad is in Barracks C, too."

The girl nodded, watching the robot. "What is it you have in mind, Electro?"

"I've concluded Blackwatch has been in business quite long enough." He crossed to the wall which was devoted to control panels, dials, levers, switches. "The first step in my overall plan calls for. . . ." He reached out, flipped a sequence of six toggles. "That takes care of all the day-shift guards, who are tucked away in the personnel compound." He cocked a thumb at a row of monitor screens. "We've just sealed all the doors on their quarters. No one can get out until these switches are switched. Now then. . . ." He unhooked a microphone. "Public address . . . let's make sure I've got Bunner's syrupy voice down pat. Sound about right?"

"Perfect," said the girl, "but—"

"Urgent! Urgent!" Electro said into the mike. "All night shift guards will leave their posts at once and report to the personnel compound auditorium. Urgent! Urgent!"

While the robot repeated the message Tad studied the picture screens. He saw guards, some with puzzled expressions, running out of the barracks buildings and away from the gates, running toward the auditorium.

"The gathering place will be seen on screens twenty-six through thirty," said Electro. "Let me know, my dear, when they've all obligingly trooped in there."

"Good seats are filling up fast," Jana said.

Electro folded his massive arms, whistled a fragment of a sea chanty. "About ready?"

"A few stragglers," said Tad.

The robot resumed his whistling.

"They're all inside," said Jana.

"Very well then." Electro threw five new switches. "They're locked in the auditorium for the night." He twisted two dials, flipped a toggle. "And so they won't be bored I'm screening some films of Supervisor Bunner's recent vacation to the Murdstone Abysmal Caverns for them."

"Can we head for the barracks now?" asked Tad.

"I'm not through flourishing, my boy." Clutching the mike, Electro made a further announcement. "All field-hands will now rise, dress and leave their barracks to rally in front of the Administration Building. At once, on the double." He replaced the microphone, fiddled with more dials and switches. "That should open all the barracks, ladies and gents."

Jana asked, "You're freeing everybody?"

"The only fair-minded way to handle the situation."

"Guess you're right." The girl laughed.

"Come on." Tad hurried toward the exit. "I want to get down there and meet my dad at Barracks B. Jana."

"Coming." She caught up with him.

"Run along, children," said Electro. "I have a few more touches to apply."

"What the hell are you doing here?"

"Well . . . I came . . . to free you . . . to rescue you."

"You still haven't gotten over that stammer. You had it when you were eleven and you still have it at seventeen."

"I'm . . . I'm nineteen, dad . . . and I don't . . . stammer."

"You're stammering right now, Tad. It's one of the most annoying things you do, that and arguing with me."

"I haven't seen you for . . . for six years. Damn it. I thought . . . thought you were dead."

"Obviously I'm not."

The workers were flowing around them. Tad had spotted his father coming out of the barracks building and run up to him.

Daniel Rhymer was a tall man, gaunt now, his skin sundried and brown. His hair was short-cropped, touched with gray. "It never occurred to you I might have an escape plan of my own worked out?" Tad's father asked him. "We've been working on a tunnel out of here for nearly three years. In a matter of weeks we'd have had it finished and then—"

"Listen to me!" Tad stepped forward, gripped his father's shoulders. They felt lean and bony through the rough-spun field-hand tunic. "Listen to me, dad. I'm not the kid you knew and I won't let you talk to me this way anymore. We thought you were dead, but then I learned you weren't. So I came halfway across this goddamn planet to get you free of here. Mom is dead and you're all I have left. But if you try to act with me the way you used to I'll leave you here and you can dig your tunnel bare handed until you die, for all I care."

His father lowered his eyes. "I didn't know . . . I didn't know she was dead," he said. "When?"

"Three months ago."

His father said, "How'd you manage to bring this off, Tad?"

"With help. A robot named Electro and a girl named Jana Taine. The three of us."

"Only three?"

"Well, we work pretty well together. And Electro's an exceptional robot, Cousin Cosmo built him originally and I repaired him."

"Yes, I remember Electro," said Tad's father. He moved back from his son. "You're taller."

"And older."

"All right." He held out his hand. "I'll try to . . . change. I'll try to like you, Tad. I can't promise . . . but I'll try."

Seconds passed, a half a minute. Tad held out his hand. "Right now we have to settle with Cousin Joshua." He shook hands with his father.

Chapter 29

Light was flowing out of the open doorways of the Administration Building, freed laborers were roaming the grounds, milling, wandering. Tad, a few paces behind his father, was heading for there.

Electro's voice came booming out of all the plantation loudspeakers. "We are running shuttles away from Blackwatch, commencing in one half hour. Plantation landvans will be utilized. Report to Cosmo Rhymer in the warehouse area at once to make arrangements."

Immediately dozens of the liberated prisoners started moving for the warehouses.

"Typical of Cosmo," Tad's father said over his shoulder, "taking charge."

They were approaching the staircase of the Administration Building. "Actually it's Electro who's taken charge, he's got Cousin Cosmo working for him."

A moderate clanging sounded inside the corridor. "My boy, I have a chore . . . Ah, good to see you again, Mr. Rhymer," the robot said. "You're looking fit, all things considered." Electro trotted up to them.

"Fit? I've lost twenty-six—"

"You'll find a bit of a reunion in progress in Bunner's late office," Electro went on. "Alice is there as well as Jana and her father. Cosmo will be there once he gets the evacuation plans solidified."

"Is Jana okay? And her dad?" asked Tad.

"All in tip-top shape, hugging, sniffing back the tears," Electro said. "Your typical joyful reuniting."

"Typical," said Tad. "Maybe I ought to meet her father and—"

"Plenty of time for that later." Electro placed a hand on Tad's shoulder. "At the moment you and I have a task to undertake. Mr. Rhymer, why don't you pop into the reunion? I've mixed up a little punch, making use of the rum tank Cosmo built into me."

"All right, very well," said Rhymer. "Tad, don't get into any trouble. I'll expect you to be back here as soon as possible." After a brief nod he went inside.

"I could have prepared you," said the robot. "Not a warm fellow, your pop."

"Yeah, I know. I remember him when we were all together on Barnum," said Tad. "But I was hoping . . . I don't know, after six years of something like this—"

"Your father is one of those admirable people who never allow their lives to be touched by what happens to them." Electro took hold of Tad's arm. "We can discuss the matter en route, come along."

"En route to where?" asked Tad as the big robot dragged him through the crowd of freed prisoners.

"I assumed you'd prefer to settle this matter yourself. We'll let your dad and Cosmo take it easy for now."

They moved into a lane which ran between two

barracks, across a flat field and up to an opaque glaz dome. Electro pressed his palm against a glaz panel and it slid open.

Inside the dome three skycars rested on the plaz floor.

"We want the blue and gold one," said the robot. "It's Bunner's and the speediest of the bunch."

"Are we going to leave Blackwatch before—"

"Only a quick jaunt, my boy. It won't take anything like the time it took us before. Hop aboard." He pointed his left forefinger at the ceiling and a large section of the dome opened to the starless night.

"What's he doing here?" Tad asked, looking down at the fog below them.

"I summoned him," said Electro. "Seemed appropriate, and it's closer than his own estate."

"Why not just get him to come to the plantation?"

"Too much unusual activity thereabouts. He'd have suspected something before he even landed." Electro set the controls for a landing on the grounds of Foghill, then put his hands behind his head. "Impersonating friend Hohl I contacted your Cousin Joshua and informed him he had to meet me at Foghill immediately. Urgent business, involving you and the fate of the entire Rhymer Industries complex. All true, by the way. Except the part about my being Hohl."

"Can we really do anything to Joshua? Prove that he—"

"My boy, I am nothing if not thorough." Electro thumped his side, causing a small panel to swing open. He drew out a thick folder of papers and faxcopies. "While you and Jana were gathering your long lost parents to your respective bosoms I was making use of all the Blackwatch computers and gadgets." He plopped the fat folder into Tad's lap. "We have enough documentary evidence to send Joshua up the proverbial river for the rest of his life."

Tad didn't investigate the contents of the folder. "You told me he's been able to buy off most of the local law."

"Which is exactly why I also used my time to contact the Interplan Law Service," said Electro. "These lads are above bribes and will be meeting us here momentarily."

"What part do I play?"

"It occurred to me you'd get a kick out of being the one to confront Joshua with the evidence of his evil deeds. Am I right?"

Tad tucked the folder up under his arm. "Yeah, you're right."

Chapter 30

Biernat, the tank-shaped robot butler, dropped his tray. "One is astounded," he said when Tad came striding into the vast living room of Foghill mansion alone. "One assumed you had—"

"That's enough blathering," said Cousin Joshua. "Clean up that spilled neococoa and get out." When the robot had complied, Joshua fixed the tinted monocle to his real eye and stared at Tad. "You've been living up to your reputation as a trouble maker, Thadeus."

"That I have." Tad crossed to the giant fireplace where his half-machine cousin was stationed.

Joshua's head squeaked as he glanced around. "And where is Hohl?"

"Flat on his ass at the Blackwatch Plantation."

"What's that? What sort of audacity prompts you to *ruzzle wurfle muzz dingle*."

Tad reached out and whacked his cousin a few

times across the chest. "Still haven't had your talkbox fixed, huh?"

"Thank you, young man," said Joshua. "I've been much too busy. Been fretting over your rude disappearance for one thing and—"

"And trying to have me hunted down."

"I might add my dear devoted sister Cornelia has taken to her bed, prostrate with anxiety over your conduct."

"Well, if that knocked her over what's going to happen next will probably finish the old girl off for good."

Joshua's monocle flipped out of his eye. "See here, Thadeus, you can't go around *muzzle duzzle furp dank dank* . . . No, I'll do it myself, you're much too rough with *wurgle burzz.*" He pounded his chest. "A Rhymer Industries product usually only needs a few gentle pats to start performing smoothly again." His metal arm creaked when he put his hand on his hip. "I'd very much like to know why you're addressing me in this rude and disrespectful—"

"Several reasons." Tad tapped the folder. "One is . . . I've somewhat grown up over the past few weeks. A little late I've been, but I'm finally about as mature as I should be at this point. More important, from your point of view, Josh, is we have a great wad of evidence against you. All the shady and illegal stuff you've been pulling off we can now prove."

"I've never done one dishonest thing in my life. If your poor departed father were still alive he could—"

"He is alive," said Tad. "We busted him free of Blackwatch. Along with Cosmo, Alice, Jana Taine's father and . . . quite a few more."

The real parts of Joshua's face grew a dappled red and then faded to a pasty white. "What you're trying to tell me is . . . the jig is up?"

"It is definitely up."

Joshua, after several tries with his real hand, located his monocle dangling from its string. He put it up to his fake eye and scowled at Tad. "You're not as mature as you think, you mooncalf," he said. "I can control almost any law officer on this—"

"Electro sent for the Interplan Law Service. They've sent a skyvan down from their orbiting satellite. Should be here at—"

"One begs everybody's pardon, sirs." Biernat came tottering back into the room. "Two gentlemen claiming to be ILS agents have arrived and wish to see you."

"Wuzzle burple zuzz," said Joshua.

Tad said, "Show them in."

The mist was spinning all around them. Tad, shoulders hunched, walked along the Foghill path. Dawn was not far off. "Okay, I'll listen," he said to Electro.

"My assumption is your father will want to return to Barnum," the robot said, wiping beads of mist off his surface. "With Cousin Joshua in the hands of the ILS someone will have to look after Rhymer Industries' affairs here on Esmeralda."

"Cousin Cosmo will do that."

"He'll need help."

"I'm sure he doesn't think I'm capable of—"

"On the contrary," said Electro. "I put in a recommendation for you before we departed Blackwatch. As you must know, Cosmo often follows my advice."

They came to the place where they'd left their borrowed skycar. "Maybe I ought to go home to Barnum, too."

"And leave all your new-found friends?"

"Such as?"

"Myself for one, first and foremost." Electro

scrambled into a passenger seat, folding his arms. "There is also Jana."

"She's . . . older than me." Tad took the control seat, got himself buckled in.

"A temporary condition, my boy. Another few years and the distance between you won't seem so great."

Tad set a takeoff pattern. "She's always talking about what a terrible person she is, about her past—"

"A defensive bit of badinage," said Electro. "Once her hubby—a first rate scoundrel, by the way, and I unearthed some splendid proof to that effect while collecting dirt on Cousin Joshua—once she's severed for good from Taine you'll see many changes in Jana."

The skycar lifted up into the misty dawn. "You've sure changed your attitude toward her."

"I've mellowed," the robot admitted. He looked across the cabin at Tad. "Are you going to stay?"

"I'm going to stay," Tad said.

Attention:

DAW COLLECTORS

Many readers of DAW Books have written requesting information on early titles and book numbers to assist in the collection of DAW editions since the first of our titles appeared in April 1972.

We have prepared a several-pages-long list of all DAW titles, giving their sequence numbers, original and current order numbers, and ISBN numbers. And of course the authors and book titles, as well as reissues.

If you think that this list will be of help, you may have a copy by writing to the address below and enclosing fifty cents in stamps or coins to cover the handling and postage costs.

DAW sf
BOOKS

DAW sf
BOOKS